PALIMPSEST

PALIMPSEST

The Future... or the Past

DENISE GUYMER

NATIONAL
LIBRARY
OF AUSTRALIA

A catalogue record for this
book is available from the
National Library of Australia

For, Stephen Jackson for the excellent suggestion for the title of the book; Rosemarie de Vries my beautiful friend for her support throughout the whole process, Guy Salvidge for his editing and suggesting the need for a stronger ending and my student Maycie who spent some time with me with ideas for the front cover.

Chapter 1

'I hope you fall over and hurt yourself Ranous!' shouted Geha, realising that she had no hope of regaining the lead. Chunks of parched clay cracked underfoot as she pursued him. Forging ahead, Ranous glanced over his shoulder to taunt Geha as he continued his reckless descent to the river. Abruptly, the crumbling path collapsed under Ranous's feet. An avalanche of clay, pebbles and youth vanished, plummeting noisily over the void. A murderous yell echoed as he and the debris crashed over the bank. Geha, who was close behind, screamed as he disappeared, and the path continued to crumble. Instinctively, she seized a small tree root protruding from the riverbank as the path disappeared from under her feet. Her heart pounded, her hands stung, and her toned muscles strained to cling to the root. Dangling, she glanced down looking for Ranous, knowing that he must still be alive as she could hear him as he cursed soundly some distance below her. She looked back up and studied the riverbank, searching for something safe to hold while her feet scrambled to find a foothold on the collapsed bank. Pebbles and soil continued to rain down on the unfortunate Ranous.

Ouref, who had opted out of the contest at the top of the bank, was now at the edge of the collapsed path, white dust swirled around her. She stood there, mouth open and observed the predicament her friends were in, unable to decide which one to help. Geha, still struggling to find a more secure position gasped, 'Ouref, can you help me please?'

Ouref shook herself and secured a firm grasp on a sturdy tree close to her and reached out, gripped Geha's hand and strained to support her weight. Geha took a deep breath and released her hold on the tree root and heaved herself over to where Ouref stood. They stood still for a moment, their backs against the bank and white dust settled all around them. Geha exhaled noisily and then looked at her friend. She giggled at Ouref, not realising that she looked a whole lot worse.

Ouref glared at Geha for a few moments and blurted out, 'You know that Erua does not like people making threats against other people – she says it is bad Geha, and now look. This is your fault,' Ouref concluded, pointing to the now nonexistent path and down at Ranous. Ouref backed away holding her breath waiting for Geha to retaliate, her eyes huge in her chalky face.

Geha sucked in her breath while she thought of an answer, for a moment mystified by Ouref's uncommon outburst.

A groan wafted up from below. Geha quickly forgot about finding a suitable retort and dropped to her knees. Looking over the side, she found where Ranous was spread-eagled across a small sapling which grew out of the bank halfway down. Geha held her breath as her eyes did a scan of his body looking for any odd angles that would indicate he had broken anything. He appeared to be fine except for a film of white clay dust and the odd pebble that rested on his body.

'Move yourself a little bit at a time Ranous and make sure you are OK, although you look fine from up here,' Geha shouted. As a novice healer, Geha was using all her skills while she observed Ranous as he tested all the parts of his body. She realised she was holding her breath while he wriggled all his limbs and then he finally rolled over the tree and hugged the bank. Geha watched while Ranous collected the skin water bag from where it had fallen into the same tree and crawled tentatively back up the bank, collecting Geha's water bag on the way. When he pulled himself over the edge, Geha examined him more closely. The three then brushed as much dust off themselves as they could. They decided that they had escaped the incident without any major damage.

With no harm done, Geha now looked at Ouref and wondered whether to respond to her accusation or not, feeling a little guilty that it may have been her fault that Ranous had fallen. Geha gave herself a mental shake and decided to give Ouref a hard glare and not pursue any further retaliation.

They were checking the water bags when Erua appeared at the top of the bank. The three younger ones breathed a sigh of relief that she had not witnessed the fall and would be unaware of the most recent disaster experienced by the three friends. Geha gave Ouref a further long glare and Ouref dropped her eyes to the ground, as Erua shuffled down to where the three friends waited. Geha saw that Erua observed the three closely and she was relieved that despite some scrutiny from Erua, she asked no questions. Geha concluded that wise women did not ask questions that had obvious answers.

Ranous picked up his water bag and turned towards the river. They skirted around the collapsed area to where it re-connected with the path and the four wended their way more sedately down to the water.

Geha dumped her water bag on the sandstone edge of the river and bent over, peered into the clear water and watched the small fish feeding on algae at the edge of the rock just below the water line. Wham! Ranous grabbed both her and Ouref and propelled them into the water. Geha had enough time to close her mouth before she slammed into the icy water. The shock of the cold popped goose bumps on every pore of her skin. She started screaming while still underwater, thinking of how she was going to get Ranous back this time, frustration levels at an all-time high. Why did boys have to be so stupid? She rose to the surface, teeth chattering, as she looked for him. He was an arm's length away as he knew that both girls would look for revenge. Geha was about to curse him but remembered that Erua was close by and the effect of her previous curse this morning made her swallow her words. Ranous looked a little disappointed when Geha rolled over and swam back towards the edge. She pulled herself over the side and onto the sandstone rock. She satisfied herself with the retort, 'You're horrible Ranous.'

'You needed a bath,' he said, 'and it is spring.'

Ouref swam back to the edge and pulled herself over the bank. The two girls peeled off their saturated tunics and spread them on the rocks to dry. Ouref and Geha both glared at Ranous who was still safely in the water. Finally, Geha decided he was right and grabbed handfuls of clean sand and started scrubbing herself from the toes up, finally rinsing her tingling body in the cool running water. Ouref and Ranous joined her in the bathing ritual, and after some time the three friends finally looked quite presentable.

Chapter 2

Erua had settled herself on one of the sandstone rocks near the edge and dangled her leathered old feet in the cool water, watching the antics of the three. Once more she pondered on the difference between Geha and Ranous and the rest of the community. The detail of their lighter-coloured hair and skin seemed to be emphasised in the early morning sun. She compared Ouref's deeply tanned skin and masses of reddish-brown hair with the other two. Geha and Ranous were much taller than any of the fully grown men of the clan, even though they were only fifteen. They also showed great intelligence and ability to understand and remember detail. Geha was her apprentice healer, and she had absorbed information with impressive skill. She sighed luxuriously and wondered what the spirits had planned for the community when they sent these two to be born of their clan.

She turned her wrinkled old face to the spreading warmth of the early morning sun and looked at the familiar surroundings of the sacred river. It was very much drier than she could remember for the many years since they had been coming here. The trees and grass which held the soil together needed life-giving rain. She breathed in the dry air and signalled a message to the spirits.

Eventually, Erua called the three to dress and they walked upstream to collect clean water. Once their bags were filled, they returned placidly to their camp careful not to spill any of the precious fluid. At the campsite the young women had already coaxed a steady flame from the embers of last night's fires. The last of the meat from the previous hunt sizzled directly on the hot stones. The delicious aroma wafted downwind to where Erua, Geha, Ranous and Ouref walked and all four recognised that their stomachs growled with anticipation as the early morning exercise had sharpened their appetite. They brought the water closer to the cooking fire and the rest of the community gathered around, sat quietly and waited for their food.

A gleaming object hummed over the treetops directly above the community. In divine terror, the clan members threw themselves to the ground to hide their faces from the Shining Ones who occasionally made themselves visible in a light so bright it hurt their eyes. The adults trembled in fear and the small children pressed hard against their mothers. Erua could observe Geha and Ranous's feet from her position on the ground. Why were they still standing? She snatched a look upwards and realised they were not only standing but also looking at the Shining Ones and waving at them. Forgetting her terror, she was now thoroughly intrigued by their reaction. When did this start happening? Erua was sure that when they were small, they showed proper respect for the gods.

Erua watched them smiling at each other as the ship hummed away. She glanced around at the rest of the clan and realised that no one else had observed that Geha and Ranous had not prostrated themselves like the rest of them. With the ship now gone, Geha and Ranous helped the older members of their clan to their feet and shushed the small children. The anxious community eventually settled to eat their breakfast, and the normal sounds returned to the camp. Erua sat deep in thought about the scene she had just observed and wondered why.

After breakfast she watched while Ranous and Geha gathered the youngest members of the community to play under the shade of the large trees along the riverbank. She sat near Ranous's mother, Sani, and Geha's mother Homatha. The three women watched Geha and Ranous with the young ones when Homatha observed, 'They will not be happy when they will have to split up for their initiations soon.'

Erua knew that Ranous would be initiated as a warrior at the next full moon. Geha was already a woman and would be initiated into the clan as an adult by the Old Mothers also at the next full moon. The three women knew instinctively that Ranous and Geha would not be happy to be forced apart as they had been born within days of each other and, despite the occasional childish arguments they had been inseparable friends since infancy.

Chapter 3

From a vantage point some distance from this scene, Ea looked at Damika. 'You know I don't want contact with the communities unless it is absolutely necessary, you know that!' he said.

Damika faced Ea and said, 'Relax Ea, if we are going to be here for a few more millennia we should have some fun.'

Ea grunted with as much derision as he could gather and looked back towards the small community. He eventually nodded to himself with as much satisfaction as was possible. A human being would have shown more emotion, the scene being so perfect. But Ea and Damika were androids and guardians of this small blue planet.

Damika increased the speed of the ship and Ea perused the land closely as they flew, searching visually for any injured animals in the area while also using the ship's surveillance sensors. He reflected that it was such a pity he had resisted so long to put this project into action. Ea had to admit to himself that he was glad that Damika had persuaded him to agree to this project, despite the difficulties they had encountered.

He reviewed his memory banks and slipped back to the Old World he had known. The Cognoscenti had known for many decades that the Old World was gravely wounded and would die if the multinationals did not conserve the world's resources. Strangely enough, at the point when all the questions had answers, Knowledge was not enough. The Old World had run out of life. The multinationals had adopted a scorched earth program for many centuries in their quest for wealth and power. The Cognoscenti knew that the world could not support the greed of the multinationals, and it seemed too late when the orders finally came to initiate a regeneration program.

Quietly however, the Cognoscenti had been planning for many years for the future and had been diverting funding to the Genesis program. Initially, they believed they could regenerate some of the Old World. Gradually, they had to accept that there was no hope, and they began their search for a new planet untouched by humans. Their dream was to create a New World only populated by people from the Cognoscenti. They had a vision to live in harmony with the environment and rule the world wisely, to only take from the environment what was necessary to live. The Cognoscenti were people from the scientific community, and they secretly developed their Genesis plan. Astronomers were involved in the search for a new planet; geneticists were recruited to collect and store genetically perfect embryos of all the animals of the world and some embryos of selected people from the Cognoscenti. Botanists collected seeds, engineers designed the androids and spaceships were designed to transport the seeds and embryos to the New World. Because there was not enough room for all the Cognoscenti to be transported to the New World, only a few of them were selected to go, and they were known as the Chosen Ones. Many years went into the planning of the project as the Old World disintegrated around them.

A planet was found, and plans were made for the journey to the New World. Calculations indicated that the new world showed a similar composition of elements that would support the different species of plants, animals and humans to be transported from the Old World. Little was known of the species of plants and animals already on the new planet, but they could not afford the time required to conduct a full-scale exploration.

The deterioration of the Old World suddenly came to a point where the citizens were demanding explanations for the breakdown of their strictly ordered world. Power cuts, shortages of food, diseases that for centuries had been unheard of were suddenly recurring and killing people; pollution unchecked, murder and small wars spiralled out of control, earthquakes, volcanoes and storms overcame the technological instruments that had kept them in check for many years. The strict order was breaking down. Conflict, pestilence and disease accelerated to the point where the safety of the project was jeopardised.

The Cognoscenti decided to send a scout ship, Genesis I, with two android guardians and a selection of all the animal embryos and seeds. As an afterthought they also added ten human embryos, genetically engineered from the most intelligent and athletic individuals of the Cognoscenti and checked to ensure that there were no mutations evident that could impact a breeding program for a small genetic group. Further spaceships would be sent as soon as they could be loaded. Just before Genesis 1 departed, the Old-World government had contact with intelligent humanoids from beyond the Milky Way, the Tartarans. They promised they had technologies that the Old-World scientists did not have access to, and assured the government they could save the planet. New hope was aroused that these people might have answers to save their planet. However, the Cognoscenti made the decision to continue the launch despite the new surge of hope.

Ea and Damika were the two android guardians selected to pilot Genesis I to the new planet. When they arrived at the New World, Ea and Damika set about building the planet in preparation for the arrival of the Chosen Ones. They seeded the world with their plant and animal species and carefully nurtured them. The plant species thrived in the new environment, having no natural predators. The animal species from the Old World took somewhat longer to establish, and the two guardians worked hard to increase the number of animals, gradually building up the numbers. Eventually, the plants and animals thrived in their new environment. The natural species and the introduced species eventually complemented each other and over millennia a new world ecology eventuated. The two guardians often noticed mutations, probably due to the different composition of soils and water. One such mutation had been with the ape lineage. One of the ape communities had grown larger brains and graduated to using stone tools, and used fire for cooking and protection. Their brain size increased, and they had a rudimentary language system. Ea and Damika observed and recorded these differences.

They also found much needed minerals which included a plentiful supply of uranium that ensured the continuation of the Old-World energy technology that powered themselves and Genesis.

A Sphinx was carved out of a natural rock at the point in the middle of the land masses. This emblem had always been an important symbol of the Chosen Ones, and it seemed natural for Ea to choose this as the marker and the place for the collection of vital information from the Old World and the New World. They carved caverns under the Sphinx to house their equipment and their bank of knowledge. A passive locator beam was installed to guide the Chosen Ones to the Sphinx, but it never recorded anyone locking onto it. They had waited many years for the fleet of ships to arrive, and they speculated occasionally about what happened to the Chosen Ones.

Ea and Damika debated about what to do with the human embryos sent with them from the Old World. Ea wanted to maintain the new world the way it was at that time and wait for the Chosen Ones to arrive. Damika wanted to grow the embryos in the labs they had set up under the Sphinx and nurture the children themselves and teach them the ways of the Old World. Ea was against Damika's idea as he vividly remembered the greed and barbarity that had led to the death of the Old World. He was very aware of the vision the Chosen Ones had for humans to grow without the Old-World values, to live in harmony with the environment and each other. He believed this was the dream of the Cognoscenti, and he wanted to carry out their wishes. Damika argued that the embryos of the Chosen Ones would have the best possible chance to grow up as caring stewards of the planet if they had the appropriate knowledge. She had been a new android when she boarded Genesis, and she had not seen the death throes of the Old World. She knew only the members of the Cognoscenti and their immaculate and luxurious quarters, and longed for the ways of the Old World as she had observed in the time she had before she boarded Genesis. She had never observed the toxic aftermath that was outside the walls of the complex.

After much discussion the two androids reached an agreement to implant the embryos into the hominid females and allow the offspring to grow and be a part of their communities. This compromise allowed Damika's request for the human embryos to be allowed to grow to maturity, and Ea's desire for the humans of the New World to be one with their world without the knowledge to abuse it. This solution was not initially without its problems however, as Ea and Damika had to capture two of the hominid females from five groups around the New World to sedate them and implant the embryos. After the implants, the guardians checked each female regularly and monitored their pregnancies – the future of the New World lay completely with the success of the project. Ea had decided if they placed the Children on different continents of the New World, it would reduce the likelihood of a catastrophe occurring and destroying all of them. Ea and Damika were then required to constantly check on their small communities around the world. The result of this close contact was that the communities began a primitive religious awareness of the two androids and their ship, an awareness fuelled principally by fear. Because of this reaction, Ea strove to avoid direct contact with the clans, and he was frustrated with Damika when she did not appear to realise the implications of these continued contacts with the communities.

She was the more human-like of the two androids and showed almost human-like emotions. Ea based his decisions on logic and felt this was the best way to solve the problems they had to address daily. Damika did not understand the reasons why he wanted to let the Children and their descendants to develop naturally at their own pace. Access to all the data would not change her opinion.

The Children however seemed to be much more intelligent than the members of their communities, and their acquisition of technological and language skills were somewhat alarming for Ea. They were passing on skills to the members of the clans and there was little that Ea could do to stop them sharing this knowledge. Damika reminded Ea that the embryos would have the DNA of the most intelligent people of the Old World, and it would be natural for them to show high intelligence. However, that did not stop her from pleading with Ea to be able to teach the Children. But he rejoiced in their innocence and steadfastly refused to allow Damika to teach them. Due to accidents, however, they had lost four of their children from two groups and they were now concerned with the survival of the last six. It was now the fifteenth year of the project.

Chapter 4

D amika broke into Ea's thoughts. 'We should check the southern sector again, the group there is very small after the lion attack last week. They will have very little ability to protect themselves anymore. We need to do something soon.'

A lioness had killed two of the Southern sector's warriors and the group was now relying on five men to hunt and defend them. Ea did not want to disturb the community but two of their Children belonged to this clan.

'What do you think should be done?' asked Ea.

'I would move the group to another clan area to their north and amalgamate them. They will be a much larger group than can usually be supported by this area, but there is enough food for them to supply everyone, including the survivors of the southern clan. There has been good rain and so there are more than the usual animals and plants in that area. That will entail the physical removal of the remainder of the southern group and transport them to the north. I know how much you wish to reduce contact with the groups, but I think we need to deal with this problem now.'

Ea was quiet for some time, and he consulted the computer banks for more data.

'The survival of the Children is of supreme importance Ea,' said Damika quietly. 'We are their guardians – we can't let them down … or the Chosen Ones.'

'You are right Damika, steer a course to the Southern Sector,' Ea instructed.

It wasn't long before the ship cruised over the last place where they had seen the group. Damika steered Genesis and circled the area. The group was nowhere in sight and the sensing equipment on board the ship was only able to detect the wild animals living in the area.

Ea decided that logically the group had taken fright and moved much faster than they had expected. However, it would also be logical that they would have moved along the river, as they would perish within three days of not having access to water. Had they moved up or down the river? It would be dark in a few hours, and they had to decide.

Ea consulted with the memory bank for a moment and then said, 'I think we will search downstream as it is in the area away from the lioness's natural territory.'

It was a good decision as they found the group within a short time with the sensing equipment aboard the ship. It was now twilight, and the group was settling for the night. Damika landed some way from the clan so as not to disturb them, aware that they did not require extra stress. Damika stayed with the ship and Ea walked to the small community to check on them. As he was observing the group from the small hill behind them, Ea heard the unmistakable warning grunt of a lion only a few metres from where he knelt. He froze. Until then he had assumed that the lioness would remain in her own territory.

The duty look-out for the clan also heard the grunt and panicked. He called out to his community who had fallen asleep because of the hard march that day. The community quickly awoke and bunched together. They fed the night fire until it burnt brightly for protection against the lethal monster that waited in the shadows.

Ea now moved with an urgency he did not possess before. He was not concerned with his own safety as he was a machine, not flesh and blood. The cat knew he was there as soon as he moved but was confused as the potential prey did not smell like the group of humans she had stalked over the previous days.

He checked to ensure that the two Children, Veran and Rhidah, were safe within the perimeter fires. He could see some of the adults as they anxiously discussed the situation and shifted themselves as close to the fire as possible. Two small children started to whimper quietly and cuddled close to their mothers. Ea searched the faces of the desperate clan and noted that one more member of the group was missing. He scanned back to Veran and Rhidah, and in the flickering flames of the fires he could see they were tense and withdrawn. The remaining men of the group had their weapons close by and noticed that the uninitiated boys were carrying weapons, including Veran.

Ea retreated to Genesis. Damika was surprised to see Ea back so promptly. 'We are going to have to work quickly Damika, the lioness has been following the group. We will have to remove her before we can move the group.'

Ea took the tranquilizer gun and they both left Genesis. The lioness was still in the same place, and she heard Ea and Damika moving close. The animal was not concerned, after all the lioness was at the top of the food chain and had very few enemies. As Ea moved closer, she rumbled a warning from deep inside her gut and bunched her muscles to attack. Ea fired the gun and within seconds the lioness was asleep. They levitated her sleeping body into Genesis. As Ea flew back to the lioness's normal hunting ground, Damika checked her and found that her leg was injured which meant she was finding it difficult to hunt her usual prey. By the time Ea had flown her back to the hunting ground, her injured leg had been repaired, and she was returned to her pride. She would quickly return to her typical habits in her own territory. It was now quite dark.

Ea flew Genesis back to the site not far from where the terrified group had made their camp for the night. The two guardians pondered the problem of moving the small community.

'We can only move ten sleeping people at a time in the ship and that would mean we would have to complete three trips to move the group and their equipment near the other community in the north,' Ea mused before continuing. 'We will sedate the entire group at their camp, and you will remain here with the sleeping ones, while I transport the groups to the north.'

'I think it will be safer for the group if you transport the warriors in the first group,' advised Damika, 'They can be transported and then woken up when dropped by at their new destination to protect the others as we move them to the new area.'

Ea nodded agreement.

Ea and Damika moved quietly over to the camping area expecting the group to be now more settled. However, the group was not aware that the lioness had been removed from the area and most of the people still talked tensely. Only the smallest children were asleep. Damika misted the sedative over the area and within minutes the whole group was asleep. The first group was levitated to the ship, and as they had decided, Damika remained behind with the others. Veran and Rhidah were amongst the first group to go.

Ea carefully selected the site for them eight kilometres from where the northern community had set up their camp. It was along a great river where the water was clear and flowing fast from recent rain. Because of this the animals had gathered and there was a large amount of food for the community to hunt and gather. There was enough food to support the extra people. He lit perimeter fires for the group, scanned the area for predators and left the first group still asleep but beginning to stir.

The ship cruised noiselessly over the northern community for a short while on the return trip and some of the warriors on sentry duty saw the ship and fell to the ground in divine fear. When the ship disappeared, several of the warriors noticed the fires that Ea had lit. The warriors decided to investigate why there would be fires in their territory.

Ea returned to a southward bearing and quickly found the campsite. Over the next couple of hours, the remaining members of the clan were transported safely to their new campsite. As the last group was transported, they were all starting to awaken, all of them confused by the remainder of the sedative and their new surroundings. One last trip was required to collect the community's belongings. Damika had gathered the tools while Ea transported the last of the group to the new area. They were treasured tools of stone, wood and bone, and formed the basis of food gathering, spiritual meaning and protection. The two guardians sighed with relief as Ea turned the ship for the final part of the journey.

Ea reflected on a job well done and the last trip back to the north did not take long. He noticed that the energy banks were low, and he would need to process some more uranium soon to replenish their power supply.

He refocused on his thoughts as he flew over the new camp. His landing lights illuminated the deadly chaos on the ground. They saw the carnage outside at the same time and Ea quickly flew the ship over the middle of the camp and hovered over the heartbreaking turmoil. Damika rushed outside to check, leaving Ea to complete the shutdown process. Ea left the landing lights on, revealing the tragic scene below the ship. At the hatch he paused, unable to comprehend the pulverised and torn flesh; a shattered white femur pointed accusingly at him. His gaze shifted to the young child whose top half of the skull had been chopped off; bone, brains and blood scattered in a bloody circle around her. Ea noticed that her hand was outstretched to her mother, their fingertips almost touching – their dead eyes connected for eternity. He looked for Veran and Rhidah, his sensors worked overtime, and he hoped for the impossible. Damika called him urgently from beyond the lit area and he hastened towards her. Her illumination device revealed the prostrate forms of Veran and Rhidah in front of some fallen trees. They had obviously been trying to flee the massacre area and had almost escaped as they were quite a distance from the rest of the group.

Damika bent down to examine the two children and realised they were badly hurt. She said, 'They are still alive, but they need to get back to Genesis as soon as possible so we can treat them.'

Ea hurried back through the place of the massacre, and he could hear the sound of death. The animals and birds had fled the scene, but the flies had woken up to partake in the unexpected feast creating a heaving, buzzing mass on the black viscous puddles forming under the remnants of the bodies. His olfactory sensor registered the acrid stench of blood and decay already occurring on this warm night. He hurried back through the carnage to move Genesis over Veron and Rhidah so they could be levitated on board, which reduced the likelihood of further injury.

After the task was completed, he hurried back to the small hospital section of the ship to help Damika. She had completed her examination of the two and administered anesthetic to treat them. Damika worked on Rhidah and Ea worked on Veran. Each set broken bones and stitched the bodies back together again.

It was hours later when the two guardians had done what they could for the two young people. Damika remained with them and

Ea returned to the cockpit to re-examine the battleground. In the daylight now he could see the full extent of the carnage.

Ea felt a deep sense of loss. For once he wished he was human, and able to respond with the full range of grief that he had observed in the Old World. He turned on the sensors aboard the ship and soon tracked the culprits. They were the warriors from the group who were camping just a few kilometres away. How could this have happened with no warning and in so little time? And why? Why?

Damika emerged from the cabin and Ea said, 'It was the clan close by who we were hoping to amalgamate our southern group with. The sensors indicate they are still moving at a fast pace about five kilometres away – running hard back to their clan.'

Ea looked from Damika to the desolation. It was not the first setback to their experiment. Ea sighed and said, 'Why does disaster and destruction seem to plague humans throughout all their history? It does not make sense.'

Damika returned to check on Veran and Rhidah and Ea began the sad labour of picking up the pieces of humanity and gather them for burial. He piled the bodies into one mass grave. Damika came out and they scattered flowers over the bodies and Ea recited prayers from the Old World. They then pushed soil over the broken bodies and returned to the ship.

Over the next twelve hours, despite the best efforts of the guardians, Veran died, and they had one more sad funeral. Rhidah continued to fight for survival.

Chapter 5

E a left Genesis as he had so many times before to work the small uranium mine. He laboured industriously for most of the day extracting the uranium and feeding it into their small enrichment plant, observing the process but not really thinking about it.

His thoughts were on the recent event, and he logically worked through the errors that had occurred to create such a tragedy. After yesterday's massacre they had now lost five of the Children. His idea of separating them on different continents had not worked, and he and Damika could not be everywhere to protect them around the world. How could they stop such things happening again? He realised that to ensure the survival of the remaining children they needed to be in one area where they could provide better protection for them. They needed a stable food source and permanent shelter. At present when the groups ran out of food in their area, Ea and Damika moved the communities to different areas where the hunting was better. He could see that Damika was correct in the need to keep them together and teach them skills that would protect them more easily. This was a major change in his attitude as previously he wanted minimal contact between themselves and humans. He considered the other options available to them, but he could see that this option was the best. They could not risk the previous day's disaster again.

As soon as the enrichment of the uranium had finished, he returned with it to the ship. He had made his decision. Ea knew Damika would readily agree to his suggestion as she had been arguing about this since they had agreed to begin the project almost 16 years before.

The hatch slid smoothly open, and the two guardians greeted each other, and they loaded the enriched uranium directly into the energy banks. Damika gave her report on Rhidah indicating that she was now out of danger and would survive with some careful nursing.

Ea nodded and then said, 'I have been considering what impact yesterday is going to have on the survival of the Children. What do you think of the idea of removing them from their communities and setting them to up to live in a small permanent community and domesticating plants and animals in their region as their food source?'

Damika nodded. 'Excellent idea Ea,' she said clasping her hands together. 'We will have to plan where to settle them. We will need a permanent water source and decide which plants and animals will adapt best to the region they will be settled in.'

The two guardians spent the next few days planning the best location to settle the community. They reviewed the best sites which would support the development of suitable plants and animals that could also be easily protected. Each location was rigorously evaluated.

Chapter 6

G eha had gone from carefree girl to disorientated woman in one day. Her feet hurt and the pesky flies sucked the sweat from her face. The thorn bushes assaulted her legs as she trudged along behind the Old Mothers. It had only been this morning when she and Ouref had been separated from their mothers and the other members of their clan when they started their journey of initiation. In the beginning she and Ouref had been excited about the journey, and they had dashed about and ran from one place to the next. They urged the Old Mothers to move faster. But now it was late in the afternoon, and Geha had run out of enthusiasm and energy. She desperately wanted to stop but the Old Mothers had said they had to get to the Women's Place before dark.

Along the way the Old Mothers shared the women's stories of the community, imparting the rules and customs everyone needed to follow to ensure the traditional ways of living continued. They also showed the girls survival techniques such as how to find water now they were away from the river, and where to find plants and small animals to survive in the harsh terrain. Geha barely took in the information. She missed her mother and Ranous. She trudged onwards.

Late in the afternoon, Geha could see a few scattered trees lining up along the horizon stretching away into the distance. Erua pointed to the trees and said, 'That is where we need to go.'

Geha's spirits rose despite the fact she was aching from the trek. How on earth did the Old Mothers maintain the pace of the journey, she wondered. I am young and fit. Geha looked towards the treeline again and felt somewhat dejected. It did not seem special, but she kept putting one foot in front of the other and finally arrived. They paused for a moment because the tree line was not the destination. Stretched out below them was a steep sided valley where a small stream meandered happily along the sandy bottom. Erua pointed out their sacred place, which appeared to be a small oasis at the foot of the path below them. Geha gathered the last of her energy and followed the group down the steep bank. On the opposite side of the valley Geha noticed where huge rocks had tumbled down in the past and trees grew haphazardly amongst them. A flock of large black birds screeched, raucously vying for the best roosting spot for the night, unperturbed by the arrival of the newcomers.

As she stumbled to the bottom of the valley Geha realised that the little oasis was a pretty spot with large leafy trees arching fingertips over a bubbling spring. A hidden chasm with tall walls of limestone stretched further downstream from the spring and the small stream continued to wind along between the walls and stretched as far as she could see. A purple butterfly drifted from daisy to daisy and tasted all their delights before she decided where to settle for the night.

'Oh wonderful,' shouted Geha, 'I would love a swim.' She started running towards the pool.

'Stop!' shouted Erua.

Geha thudded to a halt and looked at Erua with surprise.

'Stop Geha – you need to be properly introduced to the spirits who live here, and you cannot desecrate a pool, which can only be used for drinking – there is not much water out here and we need to be careful with the use of it in this area.'

Geha gazed at the pool fondly but understood the need to keep it clean and that she and Ouref needed proper introduction to the spirits. Erua and the other Old Mothers started a small fire and then gathered green branches from a tree that Geha had never seen before. 'Come over here and stand on this rock,' beckoned Erua.

The two girls moved over and stood on the flat rock which stood at the top of the chasm. It was quite cool, the sun having passed overhead hours before. The other Old Mothers hovered the green branches over the small fire and the immature leaves soon started smoking and smelled repulsive. The Old Mothers took the smoking branches and surrounded the two girls and chanted familiar songs. Geha and Ouref looked at each other and tried to stop gagging. Erua glared at the two girls and not for the first time Geha wondered how the Old Mothers endured these rituals. After what seemed ages, the Old Mothers stopped chanting, and the two girls were allowed off the flat rock. The Old Mothers then sat down and Erua said, 'Geha and Ouref you have now been accepted by the spirits of the spring. Gather the branches there and put them back in the fire and burn them down to ash.'

The girls did as they were told and then Erua announced, 'We are hungry – now go and find some food and cook us a meal.'

Geha and Ouref looked at each other – how were they to find food here? They had not been to the area before. The two girls, however, fanned out and found some familiar plants growing around the oasis. Geha assumed correctly that the Old Mothers in time past had brought plants from the river to plant at the oasis.

Ouref complained, 'I am so hungry I could just sit here and eat this without cooking it.'

Geha agreed but she said, 'I think the Old Mothers are expecting something a little better. How about I have a look in the trees over there for some eggs in those nests. You have a look for some nuts and fruit.'

Eventually, despite their weariness they cooked a meal, and they gave the Old Mothers their share and then ate themselves.

It was still early but both girls were exhausted, and Geha was happy to wrap herself in her skin, make a bed on the sand in their hut and fall into an exhausted sleep. There was no chatting between the girls that night.

It was dawn when the Old Mothers woke the girls. Geha groaned. Ouref rolled out of her skin and moaned, 'I don't think I like the idea of being an adult.'

Erua said, 'Geha and Ouref, I want you to take the ashes from the fire last night and mix it with water from the oasis and place the mixture in the holes on the rock where you were yesterday.'

Geha had not noticed the slight depressions on the rock the previous day, but she soon found them. She must have been tired last night, she thought. She and Ouref gathered the ash in a small bowl, added water from the pool and scraped the mixture into the depressions in the rock surface. The ash still smelled bad, and Geha was trying hard not to gag. The Old Mothers indicated that the girls were to lie on the rock, and they smeared the smelly mixture over their naked bodies.

Erua said, 'You will need to lie very still on this rock until the sun is high in the sky, and the spirits take pity on you and shine sunlight on your faces, and you can be reborn as adults.'

Geha quickly glanced out of sticky eyelids and calculated that it would be some time before the sun would be overhead. The rock she was lying on already felt incredibly hard and she was having a difficult time not vomiting from the smell of the ash. She decided to think happy thoughts and as much as possible thought of her life up until now and her mother and her two best friends, Ouref and Ranous. She also thought of her future – today she would know who she was to be betrothed to. She prayed the spirits would be kind and said it was OK to be married to Ranous. Geha was sure of it.

Eventually she felt the sun warming her face. The mixture had set hard on her body. The Old Mothers quietly took her hands and led her off the rock. She could not see as her eyes had been gummed shut with the ash mixture and she felt disorientated and vulnerable and allowed herself to be led to who knew where. The Old Mothers started to hum and chant. She could hear Ouref as she shuffled behind her. Geha could feel the sandstone steps and the gritty feeling beneath her feet as the Old Mothers guided her downwards. She wondered where they were going but implicitly trusted them. Finally, they sat her on a sandstone rock, and she could feel the rough sand through the film of ash on her bottom, and she thought she could smell water. Where was the water? Erua indicated that there was a lack of water in the area? The Old Mothers gently pulled her hands, and she fell forward, involuntarily giving a small shriek of surprise, firstly because she had fallen and then because she had fallen into the most deliciously warm water she had ever felt. The Old Mothers lathered some sweet-smelling soapy substance on her skin. She could feel the ash mixture dissolve. It felt so good, and she could hear the Old Mothers when they started to sing a song about being reborn and she certainly felt like she had been reborn – it was the best feeling in the world to feel clean and not have to smell the disgusting ash mixture anymore. Once more she could see and was surprised that the rock pool was quite lovely. Why had Erua not told her about this? Obviously, it was all part of the ritual. Eventually the Old Mothers were happy the two girls were now women, and they let them out of the pool.

Ouref's stomach growled loudly, and the girls remembered they had not even had breakfast, and Geha noticed there was food nearby.

She looked towards the Old Mothers, and they nodded to the two young women that they were allowed to eat. Ouref and Geha gorged themselves on the feast of fish, nuts, seeds, honey and boiled eggs. After lunch the Old Mothers spread themselves comfortably on the grass and looked at the young women. Eura declared, 'I guess you want to know who your husbands are?'

Chapter 7

Geha collapsed wearily against the branches of the huge tree seeking the wisdom of the ages through the rough bark and gazed at the late afternoon sun that peeked through the gaps in the leafy branches. She laid her head on her knees and contemplated her predicament. Soft tears slid down her cheeks and she wondered how many young women had sought refuge amongst the branches of this ancient tree over time.

Geha heard Ouref calling her name. She ignored her calls until Ouref wandered under the tree where she sat. Geha tried to stifle her sobs and moved back into the tree where the branches would hide her, but a small twig cracked and gave away her position.

'What are you doing up there Geha?'

Geha had to smile despite her sadness. Ouref had been a constant companion to both her and Ranous as they grew up. At the thought of Ranous she started to cry again but this time with heaving sobs, not the quiet despair as before. Ouref quickly climbed the tree and joined Geha on the large branch and hugged her.

'You need to pull yourself together Geha and come down out of the tree,' Ouref urged. 'Erua is looking for you.' Ouref was not quite sure why Geha was so upset. 'What is the problem Geha … please tell me and I might be able to help?'

'I don't want to marry Charthon,' cried Geha, 'I know he is the leader of our community, but he is so old and wrinkly, and Donnah has always hated me … how is she going to treat me now, I will be his junior wife … I was hoping they would let me marry Ranous.' Her face felt tight and wet where the tears had been flowing.

'They would never let you marry Ranous … you know that is not how it works Geha. Ranous is not old enough to marry and has not proved himself as a man yet … Charthon is a very good match, and he is a very good hunter … he will be able to keep you and your children well fed.'

Geha tried hard to imagine how good a match this would be, but she missed Ranous so much already and she was so repulsed by Charthon and scared of Donnah. It was well known that Donnah treated the junior wives of Charthon with spitefulness and they lived a life of misery. Also, the initiation process today revealed the information about the duties she was required as the junior wife of Charthon, which also added to her distress. She could not see anything but misery in her future. It was alright for Ouref – the elders had chosen a wonderful husband for her, and she would be the first and senior wife for him and she was very happy with their choice.

Ouref persuaded Geha to accompany her back to the camp. They climbed down and Geha wiped the tears from her eyes and washed her face in the stream.

Back at the camp Erua explained to Geha that they were to carry out a secret ritual that only the healers of the community were required to complete during their initiation. Erua prepared herself and they gathered their ritual symbols made of stone, shell and bone.

Geha followed Erua along the trail through the chasm. She tried to focus on what Erua was telling her but her thoughts were focused on Ranous and her misery. There was so many twists and turns Geha would never have been able to find her way back to the campsite even if she had taken notice of the path they walked along.

Just before sunset, Erua stopped and ascended an almost invisible game path up to a narrow ledge above the trail. Geha was curious. She followed Erua up the path and at the top was a small open cave.

Geha could feel the energy of the site and she shivered with anticipation, goose bumps rising on her skin. Geha watched as Erua lit some torches and placed them in the notches specially cut for this purpose. In the torch light paintings of sacred symbols came to life at the back of the cave. Erua brewed some tea and handed Geha a cup and urged her to drink it. It tasted nice and she quickly drank the concoction. She became fully alert and was no longer engulfed in her private misery. Erua placed the symbols she had brought with her in different positions around the cave and indicated that Geha should sit on the jasper pedestal at the front of the cave that looked towards the setting sun. Geha sat and Erua stood behind her and placed her hands on Geha's shoulders. As the last of the sun's rays dipped below the horizon, Geha could feel the warmth of the spring sunset fade and a shiver ran through her body. Erua chanted prayers and drew sacred symbols on Geha's forehead. Erua explained how the attunements she performed would help Geha to connect to the energy of the Gods. Geha slowly detached from reality and descended into a deep meditative state. She connected with her spirit guides and reached for a deep understanding of the universe. She learned many things. Her mind unleashed answers to questions she never even asked. She was grateful for the knowledge, and she saw a truth that made sense to her, and she clasped the image close to her. Eventually she could hear Erua calling her to return to the present and she struggled back hugging the answer that she never expected to receive. She struggled through the mists of her subconscious and finally returned to the now moonlit cave. Erua was there and held her close and reminded her to breathe normally. She felt disorientated and was grateful that Erua was there to wrap her skin around her for warmth. Her teeth chattered, and her skin was cold. Erua brewed a warm drink, and they ate some nuts and honey.

When Geha felt warm and contented, she had a flash of inspiration – this was where all her training during the past years was leading to, this ceremony was the culmination of all the information she had learned from Erua.

Then Erua asked what had happened in her meditation. Geha described the images that had flittered across her subconscious during the deep meditation, but not the one image that was so important. She needed to be alone to think about the full implications of the one vision. They discussed the messages from the spirits and for the first time during the initiation process Geha felt comfortable and relaxed. Erua asked her about the Shining Ones and if she had contact with them. Geha smiled and mumbled some information about the guardians. She was more focused on the message from the spirit guides and softly settled into her skin. Geha remembered the personal message from the guides in her dreams and for the first time during her initiation she fell asleep smiling.

The next morning the two women strolled back to the campsite, Geha happy to follow Erua and planned what she could do with her newfound knowledge.

Chapter 8

'I do not have to marry Charthon – I do not have to accept the decision of the elders.' Geha smiled and hugged herself, happy with the outcome of her meditation. For the rest of her time at the campsite she now had a burning desire to learn the skills that the Old Mothers taught her – she knew she would have to leave the clan if she wanted to avoid the future they had decided for her. She felt sad but knew this was the only answer. Geha had a week to learn survival techniques from the mothers. This information would be of vital importance for her future, and she constantly interrogated Erua for the information she required.

The Old Mothers were also much happier. They knew that Geha had not been pleased with their news of who she was to marry and thought she would cause much more trouble over the decision. They had their reservations about the choice as well, as Charthon was beyond his prime of life and he would need help from others in the community to support his large family in the future. But Charthon was still the strongest warrior and best hunter in the community, and he had communicated his wish to marry Geha. The choice was made at the last council of the elders before the initiation ceremonies began.

Geha knew she was safe from Charthon until the next full moon, which would be when the men returned from their initiation process. The women had one week of initiation – the men had to endure a process from one full moon to the next before they had completed their development from boyhood to manhood. One of the requirements was to kill an adult bear and then they would receive the facial tattoo, which indicated their status as a hunter and warrior in the clan. Geha constantly worried about Ranous and his journey to manhood – worried about his first encounter with a bear.

She became obsessed over the remaining days with learning the secrets of finding water and gathering plants and eggs in unlikely places and hunting the small lizards, birds, fish and frogs. Ouref could not see the benefits of learning this information and could not work out why Geha was so obsessed with this information. Erua showed Geha which plants were useful for healing during their walks. Geha had had a special relationship with Erua for many years as her novice – but her instruction was now becoming much more formal and detailed. Erua discussed the importance of connecting with the universe for spiritual guidance and healing. Geha's intelligence and natural aptitude meant she was gaining knowledge and skills quite rapidly. Erua was pleased with her student and Geha spent the last days of initiation happily absorbing knowledge.

Eventually after seven moons had passed, they began the demanding trek back to the river. Geha noticed the parched land and the birds of prey that circled overhead. The clan gathered at this part of the sacred river in spring for their initiation ceremonies each year, and after the rains there was usually abundant food available. But the spring rain was late this year, and the hunters had been struggling to provide enough food for their clan. The Old Mothers and the two young women focused on praying to the spirits for the rains to come on their walk back to the river. Geha especially prayed hard, and the trek back did not seem quite as arduous as the trip the previous week.

As the group appeared over the last hill, a small child on look-out saw they had returned, and he started yelling to the rest of the clan that the women were back. There was much rejoicing with the community when they returned and Geha was so happy to see her mother, but her heart was also longing for Ranous. The community was advised about their successful initiation and Erua informed the gathering that the young women would be married to Charthon and Yaldos the following full moon. Geha looked out of the corner of her eye at Donnah when the announcement was made, and she saw Donnah swing around and glare at her with absolute vehemence. Geha shivered despite the warmness of the day. She knew her life would be made a misery by that woman from then on. The other two junior wives looked at Geha with sympathy. They were particularly aware of how nasty Donnah could be. Homatha gasped quietly and grasped Geha's hand. Geha was reassured by the contact from her mother but was also sad to know that when she left she would not have that warmth and reassurance she had come to rely on. Geha bit her lip to stop the tears as they gushed from her eyes. But she was unsuccessful, and tears silently slid down her cheeks again. The rest of the women in the community came up and hugged the two young women and they clapped and sang the old songs to celebrate the news. They assumed the tears running down Geha's cheeks were from happiness. Donnah moved over to where Geha was standing, seemingly to congratulate her and declared out loud for the benefit of the rest of the community, 'Welcome to the family – I am so pleased you will be there to assist us in our duties.' She moved in as if to hug Geha. When she was close enough to Geha she whispered, 'And I am going to make your life a living hell.'

Geha stiffened and her eyes looked stricken as Donnah released her and moved away melting into the crowd. Geha stood silently in shock, and then she turned and ran, tears blinding her as she stumbled down the path to the large waterhole downstream from the camp. The sobs tore from her chest and her arms desperately clamped around her body; fists clenched in despair. Her breath came in deep hiccups hurting her chest. She collapsed near the roots of a large willow tree, thankful for the curtain of green that hid her fear from the rest of the world. It took an hour for her to completely compose herself. She watched the water flow past and a leaf swirled in a small eddy close by. She wondered if the leaf felt as trapped as she did. She stripped off and waded into the delicious warm embrace of the water and swam around to clear her head. She made serious plans for leaving the community much sooner than she had previously thought. As she floated, she saw the gleaming ship cruising high overhead and she felt curiously comforted by the sight of them. She also saw to the west a sight that she was looking for – it was late afternoon, and storm clouds brewed menacingly. She smiled, rolled over and made her way out of the water. She picked up her leather tunic and hastily pulled it over her head and moved up the path to where the rest of the community still clapped and sang. She joined the group of about thirty members, not wanting them to suspect she had other plans for the night. They drank the wild fermented grape juice they had made for the large ceremony due at the next full moon in celebration of the anticipated marriages and new warriors. Geha smiled knowing that leaving that night was going to be a lot easier with the community being somewhat drunk, and the storms that would come over would obliterate her footprints. It was working out much better and much sooner than she anticipated. That and the sight of the guardians hardened her mind up to escape that night.

Chapter 9

After the evening meal Geha was able to slip away undetected and she returned to her small shelter while the rest of the clan was still celebrating. The men, who had been left behind to hunt and protect the community at the river, had captured a bull the previous day. Between the feasting of meat and the consumption of fermented grapes, the singing and the general excitement of the day, Geha was not missed. She quietly gathered some food and a spare cloak. She left behind her favourite skin knowing that if she took her own it could alert the clan to her real intentions. She made her way out into the darkness in the opposite direction from where she was intending to go. She made sure her footprints were easy to spot on the short walk to the river. She then entered the water and trudged back upstream past the festivities, her bundle held high above her head. The wild sounds of revelry indicated to her that no one had noticed she was missing yet. She had lost some time doing this, but she figured that it would gain her maybe a day of searching by the clan when they discovered she was missing.

Geha progressed up the river for some hours waiting for the storm to arrive. Her teeth chattered and goose bumps popped up on her skin. She moved like an automaton and dragged her frozen body against the current of water by sheer willpower. Geha kept praying for the storm to move in, but it seemed to take forever. Continuous sheets of lightning illuminated her route up the river and thunder rumbled ominously closer and closer. Eventually a brisk breeze blew up, blowing dust and leaves over the surface of the water. She sighed with relief. Finally, it was happening.

The crash of thunder overhead jolted her senses. A bolt of lightning struck a massive dead tree about twenty paces from where she was. The tree exploded into sparks of matchwood at the base which caused the main trunk to totter in slow motion and then crash into the water. Geha stared uncomprehendingly at the weird scene. She did not realise in her exhaustion that her life was in danger. A massive wave flooded towards her, engulfing her, leaving only a short time to take a small breath before it hit. It knocked her off her feet and swirled her around in the water and dragged her violently along the bottom of the surging stream. She struck dead branches strewn along the bottom of the riverbed; rocks tore at her skin and smashed her body. She tried valiantly to swim to the surface and breathe, her lungs burning for oxygen. 'No! No!' she screamed in her head, 'Not now.' Just as lights danced before her eyes, she broke the surface of the still turbulent water and mercifully touched the bottom of the river. She propelled herself upright, burst through the water and sucked the sweet air into her lungs.

A last wave crashed into her face with no warning, and she once again tumbled into a deep pool on the other side of a sandbank. She inhaled a mouthful of muddy water and desperately thrashed her legs and searched for the bottom of the riverbed to fight her way upwards once again. A lack of oxygen impacted her energy levels, and she almost gave up the fight and let the water roll her downstream. She crashed against a submerged tree trunk and grabbed a branch to stop her descent. Geha pulled herself out of the water and over the branch. She just held onto it and coughed and struggled for breath for what seemed like ages.

Finally, the waves dissipated, and she let go of the branch and rolled onto the nearest sandbank jutting out into the river. Geha clawed her way further up the sandbank and struggled out of the water where she shivered violently and coughed up more of the water she had swallowed. The fine gravel in her mouth crunched against her teeth, and between her struggle for breath and spitting the gravel from her mouth it took some time to realise that the storm she antici-pated had arrived in earnest and the rain was drumming down on her. She opened her lips to the driving rain and rinsed the rubbish from her mouth. She then rolled over on the sand and let the pelting rain drive into her back, too exhausted to move. Her muscles felt like jelly, and she lay there in the lashing rain unable to move.

Eventually her heart rate slowed, and her brain started working and she realised she had lost her skin blanket and the food she had brought for the journey. Did she want to waste time finding them or did she need to get away from the river and find shelter making use of the rain to cover her tracks? Geha was still shivering violently from the fright and cold. She dragged her leaden and shaking limbs up off the sandbank and stumbled her way through the storm debris. She tripped over something soft and waited for the next flash of lightning to check the object. It was her skin blanket, and she was thrilled. It was saturated and completely useless to her at that point in time, but Geha laughed out loud, and for the first time she felt she was going to make it. The bursts of lightning showed her the way through the trees, and she made her way laboriously through the thick vegetation bordering the river. Geha was not fighting the rain knowing that it was her ally. She made steady progress away from the river towards the mountains where she knew Ranous was being initiated. Eventually exhausted and drenched she sank behind a large fallen tree trunk, which offered some shelter from the storm and fell into an exhausted sleep.

When Geha awoke the next morning, the sun was shining and the birds were chirping, the grass smelled clean and freshly washed near her face. Geha rolled over and groaned loudly. Her body ached badly and for the first time she could see the bruises, cuts and scratches on her arms and legs. She was also famished, and her stomach rebelled loudly. Water lay in pockets around her from the rain and she quickly drank from the cleanest puddle. She rinsed her mouth again, ridding herself of the last of the grit in her mouth.

She then looked around her to see what she could eat. A bird's nest was situated high in the trees near where she had found shelter for the night, and she scaled the tree to find four eggs in the nest. As she was climbing the birds chirped loudly and flew madly around, trying to distract her from their eggs. They then sat and sadly looked at her from the branches nearby. She apologised to the birds and explained to them that she needed two eggs to survive but they didn't seem to understand that they would still have two babies. So, she ignored them and sat in the tree slurping the eggs through a small hole she had made in the end of each egg with a twig. While she ate the eggs she looked around the country and surveyed the way she had to go. She saw the mountains to the north that was her destination and then she looked around and she could see several fruit trees over the rise. She shimmied down from the tree quickly. She grabbed her wet skin and strode to where the fruit trees were and devoured as many of the sweet berries as she could. The sticky juice ran down her chin and dripped over her hands. She licked the juice off her fingers and burped happily. She picked more for her travels and rolled them into the blanket and hoisted them over her shoulder. The ministration of sleep and food had enabled her young body to recover from the beating she had received in the water the previous night. Invigorated, she started her march toward the mountains.

Throughout the journey Geha watched where the birds were flying and found waterholes to drink quite easily. She communed with her spirit guides and used the knowledge she had learned from Erua. Despite being a seemingly barren area, the final part of her journey was much easier than the first part. She kept marching for several days and her goal became closer with each footstep. Crossing the desert close to the mountains she saw smoke rising some distance away. Instantly alert, Geha was curious. It seemed to be too small for a bushfire, and she wondered if this was the men's group. Using her tracking skills, Geha made her way to where the smoke was coming from.

Chapter 10

Closer to the spot she could hear men's voices, and she used all her tracking skills to crawl to the low ridge. Geha cautiously pulled herself over the crest and peered down. She flattened herself against the rocky ground as she knew if this was the sacred place for men that she would be sacrificed if she was discovered. Even as Charthon's betrothed she would not be spared. Geha glanced around and scrutinised the surroundings below her. The area was a deep fertile crater gouged in the surrounding desolate terrain. Small boulders had rolled down the steep hillside inside the crater, and trees and small shrubs had started growing inside where the soil had eroded, providing a relatively fertile topsoil. A small dam fed by a couple of small gullies and a spring had formed at the bottom of the crater and had become the basis of a small oasis. Many different trees, including fruit trees, were growing around the small lake and grass carpeted the ground away from the water. Birds were twittering and insects humming. It was quite beautiful, and Geha was suitably impressed with the choice of the men's initiation place. She glanced around outside the crater, and she could see the stark contrast.

Geha looked forward again and started looking for Ranous. After some searching, she found him sitting on a fallen tree facing the elders of the tribe. Hedaf was seated beside him, but she could not find Dimoa, another initiate. A small fire was burning between the elders and the initiates, and several sticks were resting on the side of the fire. Geha noticed the two initiates had fresh tattoos on their faces. Geha's heart swelled with pride and tears sprung to her eyes when she realised that Ranous and Hedaf had passed their initiation and they had just endured the tattooing process to prove they were worthy of the title of warriors. She watched until Ranous and Hedaf rose from their logs and moved towards the main group.

Geha scanned the area around to ascertain where they were sleeping so that she could find Ranous later that night. She was able to discover three smaller huts apart from the main huts. It appeared as if Ranous and Hedaf were sleeping in separate quarters from the rest of the men. This would make it easier for her to find him in the dark. She eased herself back over the edge of the crater and moved back towards a tumble of rocks a short distance away. Geha found a small cave, which had been formed by a group of boulders tumbled on top of each other. This had left a small space in which she could wriggle and have a sleep for the afternoon. She wanted to be fresh for her excursion tonight.

Several hours later Geha emerged from her hideout and consumed the last of her fruit. She was sick of fruit and started to crave some cooked food. As Geha crept to the top of the crater again, she could smell the delicious aroma of meat cooking and it was all she could do to stop from climbing down from her position and joining the men – she was starving, and her mouth was watering. She lay prone on the ground until she could see all of them making their way to the huts to sleep for the night.

Fortunately, there was only one sentry on duty. There were no predators in this area. It was so barren and isolated. Geha noted the position of the sentry and saw that he had lit a small fire at the highest point of the crater, and he was not moving around. Geha almost fell asleep a couple of times waiting for the camp to settle for the night. Finally, there was no further movement and Geha slithered down the inside of the crater towards the hut where she had last seen Ranous. As she quietly skirted around the main huts, making sure she didn't dislodge any fallen branches along the way, which would awaken the group of men. It took some time to make her way there. She finally arrived, quite proud of only having crawled into two patches of burrs along the way. She tried to pick most of the burrs out of her hand before she woke Ranous, but she was far too excited about talking to him again.

'Ranous … Ranous,' Geha whispered. She reached out and touched him on the shoulder. Ranous suddenly twitched and woke from a deep sleep, mumbling incoherently and throwing his hands around. Geha quickly put her hand over his mouth and lay down beside him to stop him waking Hedaf.

'Shh Ranous, it's me … Geha … shh, you need to listen,' whispered Geha.

Ranous was suddenly wide awake. 'Geha … what are you doing here … they will kill you … why are you here?'

Suddenly all at once Geha realised that she had not made any preparation for what she would say to Ranous, she was so focused on finding him.

'Oh!' she whispered, 'I couldn't stay with the clan any more Ranous; they told me I was to marry Charthon, and Donnah warned me that my life was going to be a misery …' Her voice trailed off and the tears, which had dried up now started again and she hiccupped and cuddled into Ranous. He pushed her away and all at once Geha was not sure she had made the right choice. What if Ranous did not want to run away with her? What would she do? – she knew that she was not going back to the clan, and she was not marrying Charthon. Ranous rolled over and started crawling out of the hut and motioned to Geha to follow. Ranous stood up and then moved stealthily from tree to tree until he was over the small hill behind the huts. Geha followed him making sure that she also did not make a sound. They squatted down behind a large fallen tree when they were far enough away from the huts. Geha looked up to the half-moon, which was showing enough light for them to see each other's faces. Ranous reached out and touched Geha's face. 'What have you been doing? You have scratches and bruises all over your face?' He then grabbed her hands, and she flinched as she still had some burrs in them. She involuntarily gasped and he turned her hands over to examine them but in the waning moonlight, he could not see.

'I have burrs in my hands Ranous from crawling down to your hut tonight.'

Ranous started chuckling quietly despite his concern. Geha was relieved as she was not certain that Ranous was happy with her decision to come to this place. He seemed to have grown so much and matured immensely. She was not sure he was the same happy-go-lucky person that she saw such a short time ago.

'I'm sorry Ranous, I couldn't accept being apart from you, and when they told me I was going to marry Charthon, and Donnah was so horrible to me when we got back from our initiation I decided I couldn't stay … and when I saw there was a storm coming I made a decision to leave … and while I was walking up-river the storm came and a tree was struck by lightning. It hit the water and started a wave that pushed me over and over and I nearly drowned … and that is how I got all the bruises and cuts …' Geha babbled. 'I'm so pleased to see you as you were the only one that I could think of to help me – but if you don't want to help me, I will just go out into the desert and live alone – I'm not marrying Charthon.'

'You are so impetuous Geha!' exclaimed Ranous, 'What did you think we could do?'

'I thought we could run away together Ranous and live in the desert,' insisted Geha. 'I learned all the things the Old Mothers taught me, and I know how to survive in the desert, and you are now a mighty hunter, and you can provide meat for us as well.'

'How did you think we would be able to leave without the trackers being able to find us,' sighed Ranous. In his initiation he had learned the basics of tracking and was aware to how well the clan hunters were at tracking – the community depended on them to track and kill animals to provide their food.

'I was able to avoid them using the river and the storm,' boasted Geha. 'Oh! … does that mean you are coming with me Ranous?'

'It was obvious that their best trackers were not tracking you Geha and you were lucky with the storm,' he argued.

'I know … but the guardians gave me a sign before I left – I knew I was going to survive. And I know I will … So, are you coming with me?' Geha looked cheekily from under her lashes at Ranous making his heart skip a beat.

Ranous sighed, 'You will need to give me some time to think about this Geha. This is a huge step. I hadn't even considered it.'

'I'm sorry Ranous … I will leave you now and I will wait for you to make your decision, but I can't wait too long as I need to get away, especially if you are not coming,' Geha sighed. 'You will need to let me know by tomorrow night … I will come back here tomorrow night.'

Sadly, she turned, and with tears in her eyes stumbled away, and with less care than she had shown when arriving, returned to her cave. Geha finally fell asleep towards dawn and slept late into the morning.

Chapter 11

When she awoke the sun was high in the sky. Her stomach growled and she realised she had forgotten to ask Ranous for some food. She was out of fruit, and although she was sick of fruit yesterday, she would now have been extremely happy to eat it or anything else she could find. Geha knew where to get water still but the only place where food was available was back in the crater. Geha thought she might have been able to trap a lizard in the boulders, but they seemed to have moved deep into the rocks where she could not get to them.

She tried to ignore her hunger but eventually she decided to crawl back down to the crater and find some birds eggs. She knew she was tempting fate to venture out during the day. She had slept in and therefore did not know which way the men had gone that day. There was not a great deal of cover for her to use to get to the crater and she was scared stiff in her short sprint to the edge. Her legs trembled with fear, and she held her breath for the short dash. She threw herself down flat on the ground at the crater's edge and looked around surreptitiously, her heart thumping furiously. Geha then pulled herself over the edge of the crater and hid behind a group of boulders clustered around the top. She rolled close to the shade of the boulders and stayed there until her breathing slowed to a normal pace and her hands stopped trembling. She then pulled herself around the corner of the boulders and looked around the area. There were no human sounds, just the usual bird and insect noises. All at once she realised that the men were not in the area, and she was free to explore. She relaxed, sighed and then giggled to herself about how melodramatic her entry into the crater was. She immediately looked to where the men were keeping their food away from the insects and ants under the shade of a large tree. She dashed over to the food storage area and pulled the leaves off the food. Her mouth was watering. She had to laugh when she saw that it was not only meat from yesterday's hunt, but also fruits, vegetables and eggs. All foods that men would not demean themselves to gather in front of the women. It was women's work, and the men pretended that they would not know how to gather such food as they were mighty hunters. Geha wondered if it was the job of the new initiates to gather the fruit, vegetables and eggs. It didn't matter; she was starving and started feeding herself as quickly as possible.

Finally, she was satisfied. She could not eat as much as usual as she had not had access to regular food since she had left the clan. She grabbed some of the strips of bark and started to pile some of the food onto it to carry with her for later. She was concerned that the men would notice some of the food was gone and tried to arrange it to make it seem as if the quantity of food had not decreased.

Suddenly she heard something that chilled her to the bone. She gasped and stood bolt upright and tried to determine what the noise was. As she stood straining to hear what had interrupted her, she was finally able to hear men talking indistinctly not too far away. Geha quickly gathered the food and moved away in the opposite direction from the sound of the voices. The fear was suddenly back, and she started cursing herself for being so stupid. Breathing hard she sprinted to the boulders before the men appeared over the edge of the crater on the opposite side. Geha threw herself down behind the boulders near the top, just as they appeared over the edge. Her breathing was ragged, and she was sweating with fear and the sudden surge of adrenaline. Oh! Why was she so stupid – no wonder Ranous did not want to go with her. She lay there, gasped for breath and her heart pounded, mouth dry. After a few moments of recovery, she rolled over to examine the scene. The men had arrived at the food shelter with a small dead animal. They were in a happy mood and celebrating and congratulating each other. Hedaf coaxed the embers into a flame and started to feed the small fire. They prepared to roast the animal for the evening meal.

Geha was quite relieved to see that they didn't seem to notice their food storage had become somewhat depleted. Wonderful – it seemed as if the spirits had saved her again. She decided to move away and back over the crest of the crater. She crawled slowly and dragged her food with her on the piece of bark. She constantly glanced back over to shoulder to see where the men were, and therein lay her downfall. She didn't notice the small boulder in front of her and when she thrust her hand forward, she suddenly dislodged it, and it started rolling down the slope. She tried to stop the rock, but it was moving too fast, and it started to dislodge more stones and suddenly a mini avalanche was in full flight. She froze and then glanced behind her. The men were looking up the slope towards her and she was in full view.

All at once the men knew that a woman had invaded their sacred space, and they gave a shout and picked up their weapons. Geha knew the full implications of her actions and jumped to her feet and started to sprint out of the crater. She didn't look behind her to see where Ranous was, he would have to make up his mind about whether he was with her or not. She dropped her food supplies. Flight was the only way to survive. She did not have time to think she just ran. She knew that she had to keep in front of the men and their spears. She tore off down the slope in the same direction in which she arrived. At least she knew the lie of the land this way. She knew that there was a small ravine some way off where she might be able to hide. She was not sure if the men knew about it but she was sure she would die if she stayed where she was. She was fit, and the years of living with the clan had honed her muscles. She was running as hard as she ever had. She was also aware that the men who chased her were much fitter and faster. She focused on the task ahead and tried not to look back, but she needed to know how close behind they were.

She was startled to see that Ranous was way out in front, and a small sob erupted from her as she wasn't sure whether he chased her to capture her or whether he intended to join her to leave the clan. She couldn't be sure, so she accelerated across the dangerous boulder strewn terrain. She risked another look behind and noticed that Ranous had gained on her and Hedaf was not too far behind him. One of the elders had fallen over a boulder and had injured his ankle. The others had pulled up to help him and shouted encouragement to the two young men who now chased Geha.

Geha began to feel the pressure. The initial adrenaline surge was now over, and her breath came in ragged gasps, and her legs felt weak. Ranous started shouting at her, 'Keep going Geha – don't give up – I'm coming with you.' Geha drew her breath in huge sobs, and her body began breaking down. She spun around to turn back to Ranous.

He kept shouting, 'No! No! Go on … don't stop … keep running.'

Geha stopped, not sure what to do. All at once Hedaf realised that Ranous was not chasing Geha for capture, and he stopped and raised his spear. He threw it and it curved in a flawless arc snaking perfectly towards Ranous. Geha screamed when she realised what was happening, 'Look out Ranous … there is a spear.'

Ranous jerked to one side, but the spear thudded into his thigh and hurled him to the ground. Geha screamed loudly, her hands shot to her mouth, and she started to run back towards Ranous, not caring for freedom if she could not share it with him. Hedaf was now unarmed. He ran back to the men and shouted for help from the others. They could not work out what had happened and just assumed that the two initiates were capturing Geha. They could not imagine that Ranous had gone against the clan laws.

Geha ran back to Ranous and examined the spear sticking out of his leg. He had grabbed his thigh and groaned loudly. Her heart was in her mouth not sure of what she could do. Then she heard a familiar sound, and she looked up at the sky. The guardians made their way towards the distressed couple. Geha looked back towards the group of elders and Hedaf and watched them transfixed by the shining spaceship and they dropped to the ground and prostrated themselves in the dust shielding their faces from the frightening sight. Geha then felt herself and Ranous being levitated slowly into the belly of the spaceship and the hatch slid shut. Genesis then banked to the right and sped off towards the sun.

Chapter 12

The door slid open to the cockpit area and Ea looked around. Damika smiled and said, 'The operation was a success. I have been able to remove the spear from Ranous's leg, and he should be completely recovered in a few weeks. I have given him some antibiotics, and he is a bit groggy from the anesthetic and pain killers, but Geha is sitting with him now … I'm guessing that this is a perfect time to start our new project. I have not introduced Rhidah to them as she is still recovering. I think it would be best if they do not know each other yet. Ranous should be well enough to leave the ship in a day.'

Ea nodded agreement. Damika continued her surveillance of Ranous for another twelve hours. Geha stayed with Ranous learning more healing techniques from Damika, and Damika was impressed with the healing knowledge that Geha had. Eventually they were satisfied Ranous was out of danger and that Geha's healing skills were competent enough to nurse him back to health.

Ea moved Genesis on a westerly route and in a few hours cruised to a halt beside a group of caves. Ea hovered the ship between the cave and a beautiful stream tumbling over a waterfall into a clear pool with a sandy bottom. The pool was fringed with trees and rushes, and Geha looked into the water and could see fish swimming lazily around. She was mesmerised by the peace and beauty of the spot. She could not wait to have a swim, and looked wistfully at the pool. All four disembarked, and Ea and Damika slowly walked with Ranous between them towards the cave.

Damika noticed that Geha was enthralled by the beauty of the location and said, 'Ea and I call this place Eden.'

Geha nodded absently and followed them reluctantly looking back at the delicious looking water and suddenly the image of this scene replayed in her mind from her meditation. This was the place she was promised by the spirits.

Inside the cave was a big roomy area with a sandy floor smelling clean and fresh. Natural light filtered down from a vent in the roof of the cave. There was a wooden table and chairs and a few beds, each with a mattress and blankets that were not animal skins. Geha and Ranous had never seen such wonders before and had to wait for Damika to demonstrate the use of the furniture. Ranous lay down on the bed as his leg was beginning to throb. Damika moved over to Ranous and gave him some pain killers, and he was soon asleep.

'You will need to give him more of this when he wakes up,' said Damika, 'Leave the bandage on his leg and we will be back tomorrow. There is a small freshwater rock pool at the back of the cave and there are cups, plates and bowls over on the rock ledge. There are water containers for collecting water. Fruit and nuts are available on the trees outside. We have set up a fish trap down the river and you could check to see if there should be something in it to eat for dinner. If you need us before we are scheduled to return you can press the button on this device.' Damika handed her a metallic device and then they left.

Chapter 13

Geha sat down beside Ranous and looked down at him, her heart bursting with love. She soothed his brow and then lay down beside him and curled up and fell into a deep sleep, the first she'd had in many weeks. The stress of the last few weeks had taken its toll.

Ranous only stirred once during the night and Geha gave him the pain killers and a drink of water, and he returned to a deep sleep.

She eventually woke to the sunlight as it streamed through the vent onto their bed. Geha woke with a start and looked over at Ranous who was still asleep. She eased herself away from his body and rolled off the bed. She stretched and walked across the floor to the mouth of the cave. Geha paused and took in the perfect scene. The beautiful trees where birds twittered in the branches and the waterfall gushed exuberantly into a sparkling pool. Geha sighed – it was paradise. She sent a message to the great spirit to thank them for her wonderful new home. She turned her face to the early morning sun drinking in the serenity. She knew that she should gather some food for breakfast, but the pool beckoned to her. Geha walked down to water and pulled off her tunic and slid into the cool sensuousness of the pool. She released the tension of the last few weeks as she glided and threaded her way through the aquatic wonderland. She eventually scooped up a handful of sand and picked some leaves from a soap wort plant and crushed them in her hands. Using the sand and the leaves she made a lather and scrubbed her bruised body carefully. She ran her fingers through her hair detangling the knots that were evident from lack of grooming and lathered her hair with more of the leaves. She stood under the waterfall which massaged her aching muscles and rinsed her hair.

Chapter 14

Ranous woke and looked around the cave. Where was Geha? His thigh was sore, and he was hungry. He rose painfully to his feet and, using the wall of the cave, struggled outside. Unlike Geha, he didn't notice the scenery outside; he was focused on his pain levels. His thigh was burning, and he felt his stomach tighten and acidic bile rose involuntarily into his throat. A cold film of sweat appeared on his skin, and he slumped onto a rock outside the cave and leaned against a small tree growing near the rock. He closed his eyes and rode the waves of pain until they started to recede. After several minutes he felt able to reopen his eyes. He refocused on his surroundings and soon saw Geha under the waterfall. He relaxed and feasted his eyes on the sight of this beautiful woman. His leg throbbed, and a twig stuck uncomfortably in his back, but he pushed the pain to the back of his mind and let the early morning sunlight and the sight of Geha enjoying her bath lull him into peaceful somnolence. He started to imagine being with Geha and dreamed of a life with her.

Eventually Geha completed her ablutions, and she turned and was startled when she looked around and saw him. Ranous smiled.

Geha smiled back. Ranous watched as she waded through the water to the edge of the pool and pulled herself over the edge. She picked up her tunic and walked back to where he was sitting. Rivulets trickled down her skin running between her breasts and over her stomach and down her legs. As she moved closer to him, she used her tunic to wipe some of the water away. Ranous was captivated by the sensuousness of the movement. Geha smiled at Ranous and squatted down beside him to check his bandage. Her hair brushed against his chest as she bent down to check his thigh, her fingers brushing against the hairs of his leg. Ranous held his breath, his hypersensitive skin screaming for the sweet touch of her fingers. He moved his face so he could watch her checking his leg. She bent her head upwards and saw him looking intensely at her. Their eyes locked and her smile vanished. Geha seemed to glide upwards until her head was level this his. She brushed her lips with his. It was all he imagined it to be. She tasted like honey, and he moved his hand up behind her head and tangled his fingers in her wet hair pulling her up towards him, kissing her, tasting her, smelling her deeply. His body responded with every fibre of his being, and he thought he was going to burst. He started to tremble and grasped her closer. Geha lost her balance, and she collapsed on top of him throwing her hand out and connecting with his thigh. Ranous suddenly re-lived the pain that he experienced when the spear first struck him. A burning sensation tore through the centre of his thigh and a torturous scream erupted from his lungs and he collapsed in a writhing heap on the sand, the pain immobilising him.

Geha gasped and started crying, 'I'm sorry … oh my God … Ranous I'm so sorry … are you OK?'

Ranous could not reply. He was sucking in air and folded into a foetal position, groaning loudly, tears rolling down his face. Geha ran into the cave for more painkillers and a cup of water. She helped Ranous take the medicine and then she checked his bandage. There didn't seem to be any fresh blood coming through and she lay on the ground cuddling him until the pain receded. Eventually Ranous could feel the pain killers working and his body relaxed. To divert attention from himself he said, 'I think we need some breakfast Geha … can you find something to eat please before I starve.'

Geha expelled the breath she had been holding. 'Trust you to think of your stomach – I thought I had killed you. Do you want to go inside, or do you want to stay out here?' Ranous indicated that he wanted to stay with a wave of his hand. She then went and picked some fruit and nuts off the nearest fruit trees. They feasted off the bounty and sat back in the sun contented with life.

Ranous, despite appearing to be much better, did not think that he was strong enough to be moved and he declared, 'I like being out in the sun. This place really is amazing, isn't it?'

Ranous fell asleep and Geha went searching for something for lunch.

Chapter 15

Ranous awoke to the smell of food cooking and realised that he was absolutely starving. He rolled over towards where the delicious aroma was coming from. His hand tangled in a rope, and he noticed that Geha had set up an awning with the blankets to prevent him being sunburnt. He smiled and said, 'Thanks for looking after me. What are you cooking? It smells delicious.'

Geha squatted beside the heath that she made from rocks and flat stones. She checked on the fish in the banana leaves and said, 'About time you were awake – I found some fish in the traps in the river, so I thought it was the best idea. It's ready if you are hungry.'

Ranous nodded. Hungry? He was ravenous!

Geha lifted a large chunk of the fish and some of the vegetables onto a plate and brought it over to where he was lying and set up lunch for them.

'How are you feeling?' asked Geha.

'Brilliant … and starving – thanks, this is great,' responded Ranous between mouthfuls.

After they had eaten Geha removed the remains of the meal some distance away for the ants to demolish and squatted down beside Ranous. They had not been able to talk since being rescued as Ranous had been in too much pain and it was difficult to talk with Ea and Damika around.

She said, 'I wasn't sure when you were chasing me that you were coming with me or whether you were trying to kill me ... when did you make that decision?'

'Subconsciously I think I knew that I was always coming with you, but you turned up so unexpectedly and I didn't have time to think about the future. Hedaf and I had just completed the bear hunt and got our tattoos, so we were thoroughly connected as brothers, especially when Dimoa was mauled by the bear on the hunt and had died several days before. We had tried so hard to save him ... it was terrible,' reflected Ranous sadly.

'Can you tell me about it please?' pleaded Geha.

Ranous looked over at her, looking so vulnerable but knowing that she needed to know the story. He also thought about the decrees they had received from the elders about women knowing about their secrets. It would be bad luck for the whole community for women to know about the men's business. But he remembered that they were no longer part of the community.

Geha thought he was not going to tell the story and prodded him.

'Are you going to tell me or not,' she prompted.

He smiled and nodded, 'Where do you want me to start? Do you want to know the whole time since we were away, or do you just want the bear story?'

Geha thought, 'Just the bear story ... we have our whole lives to tell me the rest. I'm curious as to how Dimoa came to die?' she inquired.

Ranous breathed deeply as if he needed the extra oxygen, closed his eyes and started. 'The elders took us on a march to a forest north of where the crater is. It took many days for us to get there. Along the way we had many opportunities to practise using our spears for hunting and the warriors had organised us to work as a team to be able to hunt and kill a bear together using our spears. It seemed just a game at the time as I had never seen a bear before then … just listening to the stories of the men before we went on the initiation … it really didn't sink in that we could be on a life-or-death mission.'

Ranous took a sip of his water and settled back into a more comfortable position against the rock. The painkillers were working, and he started relaxing. He then continued.

'We were all walking along in single file along an old game track. The older men had walked in the dense forest before and were giving us initiates a hard time as we were so amazed by the height of the trees in the forest and how cool and close together all the vegetation was. You should have seen it Geha, the trees were twice the height of those along the river like we are used to, and the smell was wonderful, and it was fresh enough to clear my nose. So, we were relaxed and enjoying ourselves without a care in the world. We were heading towards the caves where we were to do paintings and ask the gods for their help to hunt a bear for our ceremony. The elders had already collected the different coloured ochre for the painting from different sites along the way to the forest and they were carefully carrying the ochre in small bowls. They told us we were not allowed to carry the ochre for them because we were still not initiated. But I really think they were more concerned that we were too silly and mucking around too much to be given such an important job. We would have a day's march to go back and get more ochre if someone had spilled it. When we were a certain distance from the caves, Thordam started chanting a song to warn the gods we were coming. It was quite eerie, and I remembered that a shiver went down my spine. It must have had the same effect on Hedaf and Dimoa because we all stopped being stupid and quietly formed a line behind Thordam. He was chanting this song and doing a little dance as we walked up to the cave where we were to have the ceremony. There were some bushes over the opening of the cave and Thordam was having some problems getting himself and the ochre through the opening of the cave. Dimoa moved in front to pull some of the bushes away to make it easier for Thordam to enter the cave. Behind the bushes was the biggest bear I had ever seen – it was the only bear I had ever seen but it was huge all the same. It rose on its back legs and let out a roar that came from its toe nails and I could smell its foul breath from where I was. I was glued to the ground, my brain was too shocked to comprehend the situation, and I suppose the others were having the same problem. The bear was bigger than Dimoa when standing and it reached over towards him and grabbed him with its claws and then sunk its teeth into his head and neck and started to shake him and you could hear it biting chunks of flesh off his head and back. There was lots of blood and flesh flying everywhere and Dimoa screamed and screamed, his legs were kicking everywhere but he had no hope of getting away from the bear. Thordam had dropped the ochre everywhere and all sorts of colors were being ground underfoot by the bear and Dimoa and Thordam. Thordam, I remember, was scrambling around on the ground trying to pick up the precious ochre, not thinking about his safety at all. The warriors were the first to react, but they were at the back of the group. They raced forward and grabbed Thordam and the other elders and pushed them away from the bear. Hedaf and I were now the only ones close to the bear as the warriors were still pushing the elders away from it. The bear was snuffling and growling as it chewed on Dimoa's head, and he was still screaming and kicking. It took a while for me to react despite the training the warriors had given us. But I finally looked at Hedaf and we picked up our spears and advanced on the bear – it was quite easy as it was fully occupied with eating Dimoa. But the difficulty was that it was in the mouth of the cave, and it had hold of Dimoa and was using him as a shield to stop us getting to him. Hedaf and I split up and approached the bear from opposite sides, spears ready. I felt quite calm at that stage, and I was only reacting to the situation as we had been taught. I could see Hedaf on the opposite side of the cave rushing towards the bear, spear held in front of him. We rushed together and jammed the two spears into the body of the bear. I was quite surprised at how difficult it was to push the spear into the flesh of the bear – it was like trying to pierce a rock and I couldn't get the spear far enough in to hit a vital organ. However, the bear grunted with surprise and dropped Dimoa. Dimoa stopped screaming but was now groaning and bleeding on the ground, making it difficult for Hedaf and me to get a good position to attack it. The bear now ignored Dimoa and looked around with its horrible, beady little eyes. It had blood dripping down its front and chunks of Dimoa's flesh were hanging off its teeth as it swung its head from side to side trying to decide which one of us to attack. As Hedaf seemed to be the closest at the time it roared at him and lunged towards him. Hedaf sprang back and I again attacked it from behind, again only making him more ferocious as I could not get the spear in far enough to mortally wound him. The ground was slippery from the blood and made it difficult for me to get a good enough grip to push forward. He then sprang back towards me stumbling over the wounded Dimoa, looking at him, but then deciding to attack me instead. It roared again and dropped to its four feet and lunged at me. I anticipated that it was coming for me, and I jumped back away from it. Hedaf then also attacked it from the rear and like me had a great deal of a problem trying to get the spear into its body. It just seemed that we were infuriating it more and more and none of the hits we were making on the bear seemed to be weakening it. There was a lot of blood on it, but I think it was mostly Dimoa's. I was starting to shake from the adrenaline surging through my body and Hedaf and I were working as a team thrusting our spears into the back of the bear while the bear was attacking the other person. I was fully absorbed by the effort; there was no time to think about other things other than killing the bear. It was fully absorbed in killing us – it would be either us or it. The bear was pushing us slowly back towards the path and I wasn't looking behind me and I stepped backwards and could not feel the ground. My leg collapsed under me, and I stumbled backwards into nothing falling flat on my back. The bear sensed victory and lumbered towards me growling madly, his foul breath and yellow teeth coming closer and closer. I was still holding the spear in front of me and as I fell had the presence of mind to hold onto it. The bear leapt on top of me and landed on the spear as it came down. I was crushed by the hairy body, and it weighed as much as Hedaf and me together. I couldn't breathe and there was no way that I could have got away from under the bear by myself. When it seemed as if I was going to die from suffocation and the bear was twitching and convulsing grinding me further into the ground below, Hedaf and the others eventually pulled the body of the bear away and I was able to breathe. I just lay there on the ground sucking in great gulps of air until I was finally able to talk. Geha, I think I had a couple of broken ribs from where it fell on me, and it hurt every time I breathed. It still hurts a bit even now. I rolled over and struggled to my feet. By the time I hobbled back to where Dimoa was, the rest of the group were gathered around him. Thordam was bent over Dimoa muttering prayers. Dimoa was groaning and you could hear the gurgling while he was breathing. It was quite terrifying not knowing what to do. Thordam was gently replacing the flaps of skin on what was left of his face and back.

Charthon looked at me and confided, 'He has deep cuts and lost a lot of blood. I'm not sure if he will survive. Most bear attacks result in a bad fever and eventually death.'

Ranous took a drink from the cup and then continued his story. 'Thordam then motioned to the warriors to pick up Dimoa and carry him into the cave where the bear had come from. They lit the torches they had brought with them for the ceremony. We moved further back into the cave and around a couple of corners we saw where the bear had been living. There were a lot of bones scattered over the sandy floor. We continued through the cave and eventually came to a large open area. The warriors held up the torches and we could all see the paintings on the wall of the cave. In the flickering torchlight they almost looked like real animals moving. It would have been almost unbelievable to see in different circumstances, but we were focused on saving Dimoa. The warriors put the skins on the ground and laid him down on them. Thordam sent his apprentice out to look for the plants to sooth the pain and reduce Dimoa's anticipated fever levels. Thordam then started chanting and then the rest of us started chanting as well. Sometime later the apprentice returned with the herbs and Thordam ground some of it and mixed it with water and dribbled it into Dimoa mouth. The other leaves were rested on the deep gashes on his face, back and shoulder. For several days the men took it in turns to eat, sleep and chant. We were eating the flesh of the bear, so we didn't need to hunt, and just finding some berries close by kept us in food. Thordam is an old man, but I don't think he had much of a break at all during those days; it was amazing that the old man was so resilient.'

Geha remembered how tough the Old Mothers were on her initiation and could only nod in agreement.

Ranous continued the story. 'After about three days the fever really set in and Dimoa was hot and sweating and shaking. You could see the pus oozing under the crusted scabs and you could smell the rotting flesh, but we kept on with the medications and chanting. Dimoa finally died after four days, and we buried him there at the cave with the bones of the bear. He was buried with full honors as a warrior. It was very sad, and it was a highly emotional time for both Hedaf and me. So, you can probably see why it took some time for me to decide to come with you. We had only just got back from the hunt, and we were still grieving Dimoa's death, and we were blood brothers. We had survived an extraordinary event. I'm sorry, but at the time I was only thinking about the present. The past and the future were a long way from where my thoughts were.'

Ranous turned and looked at Geha for the first time since he started telling the story. He was not surprised that her eyes shone with tears. She leaned over and kissed him gently on the forehead. He had expected that she would be angry but not sure now why he would have thought that. He gulped the rest of the cup of water and sighed deeply. He realised that his hands were tightly clenched, and he deliberately unlocked his fingers one by one, closed his eyes and breathed deeply for several minutes, slowing his racing heartbeat. Genesis cast a shadow over the usual spot and Ranous took a deep breath and a sip of water.

Chapter 16

Geha jumped up and strolled over to where Genesis was hovering, waiting for Ea and Damika to disembark. The hatch yawned open, and Geha stared in shock at the sight which met her eyes as the group slowly levitated to the ground. A third person was standing between the two guardians and even more of a surprise was a wolf cub cowering on a leash behind Damika. Geha did not know which way to turn. She felt trepidation about the extra person, but some deep maternal instinct wanted to rush forward and cuddle the little wolf. She could see he was emaciated and would need much care to bring him back to health. Geha moved closer to examine him. Damika handed her the leash, and she pulled the cub towards her. He resisted with as much strength as his puny little body could muster. He pulled and tugged at the leash, whimpering softly. His distress was evident, and Geha's heart was aching to cuddle him but knowing that this would increase his misery even further.

Ea and Damika moved forward with the young woman between them, supporting her as she limped between them. Geha then realised that she too was very much in need of nursing care, and she instinctively started her scanning process she used to determine what injuries she had and what care she needed. Geha noticed that she had stitches to her head and a sling for her arm as well as the injury to her leg. She also sensed there was a lot more internal damage and that her return to good health would be a long process.

'Geha,' said Ea, 'I would like you to meet Rhidah. She was involved in a serious accident several weeks back and Damika and I noticed your healing skills with Ranous. We have made the decision to bring her here to recuperate. We think it is best that she is here with you and Ranous at Eden. We don't think being on the ship is the best place for her to be now. We are sorry we did not introduce her to you while you were on board, but we felt that was the best for all involved. We need to sit down with everyone here and discuss what is going to happen to this community. Several incidents have now happened to make us realise that we need to bring all the young people to Eden.'

Geha was confused by his words but decided to wait until they had returned to where Ranous was waiting before she interrogated him. The three of them shuffled towards the cave, and Geha pulled on the cub's leash until they arrived at the place where Ranous was sitting enjoying the sun. Geha watched Ranous's eyes open, and his face turned to amazement now that he could see Rhidah. Ea and Damika settled Rhidah in the shade against a rock close to Ranous. Geha strode over to Ranous and handed the cub's leash to him, his mouth dropping open even more. The cub scooted under a bush beside Ranous, as far as the leash could extend. Geha hastened inside the cave and picked up a dish and filled it with water and placed it in front of the little wolf cub. He cringed as low as he could get under the bush trying to avoid any contact. She then dashed over to where she had left the remains of lunch and picked up chunks of fish and shook the ants off. She placed these bits of food in front of the little wolf cub. He snuffed at the air and was suddenly interested in the food. Inching out of his hide he gulped at the fish hungrily. The others watched fascinated as he searched for more crumbs, and having a drink from the dish went back to his safe place and watched the people. Realising he was not in any immediate danger, the cub closed his eyes and dozed off to sleep, forgetting he was supposed to be scared. Everyone remained quiet watching the little cub during this process, feeling happy now that he appeared to be more relaxed in his surroundings. Ranous attached his leash to the bush he was sleeping under.

Geha then collected three cups of water for the humans and some fruit and nuts. With the cub now settled, the three young people turned to Ea and Damika silently asking for answers to their questions.

Ea began. He explained the history of the Old World and the process of getting the new planet ready for the Chosen Ones, always expecting them but never having had contact with them since they had left. He explained that there were two other young people the same age as them in another part of the world. He also explained why they now had decided to gather all of them in one safe place and to domesticate plants and animals for food. The little orphaned wolf cub was accidentally the first animal in this process. Damika had spotted him slumped beside the lifeless form of his mother in their flight over the southern sector that morning. On the spur of the moment, she levitated him into Genesis and both Ea and Damika had spent some time trying to capture him in the ship and tying a collar to his neck and attaching a leash.

Geha looked at the little cub now sleeping peacefully under the bush and looked at the others whose gazes were also riveted on the cub. 'I am happy that you decided to bring him here Damika. He is very sweet.'

There was much more to talk about, but the two patients looked very tired and there was only so much information that the three young people could take in. Even Geha felt exhausted by the overload of information. Damika checked Ranous's leg and gave instructions on what nursing Rhidah required. In the late afternoon Ea and Damika resumed their guardianship of the rest of the planet and the three young people set about re-organising their small part of the world. The little wolf cub watched the people from under the bush he had hijacked. His furry little ears checking the sounds of humans and his eyes missed nothing.

Geha started dinner and the little cub suddenly remembered the delicious aroma of fish and inched across slowly now at the very end of his leash straining to be closer to the luscious smells. Geha noticed his interest and fed him the skin and guts from the fish she was cooking. He gulped down the food and stayed where he was, not retreating under the bush that had been his hiding place most of the afternoon. Geha was also watching him and finally said, 'I will name you Oonie … a good name for a wolf cub.' Rhidah and Ranous, who were also watching Geha cooking, smiled and agreed it was a very good name.

Geha noticed that Rhidah looked exhausted and quite shy in the presence of herself and Ranous. Much had happened to her in the last month, and Geha could see she was having great difficulty in accepting her new reality. Geha glanced at Ranous who also seemed confused with the new circumstances. Geha examined her own feelings, and she had to admit that she felt a little cheated that she and Ranous were not to be the only inhabitants of Eden, but she cast her mind back to community living in the clan and realised that she did feel somewhat isolated without the busy community life. She glanced back at the two people and a little wolf cub who were relying on her skills as a healer and mentally shook herself to return to the present. The little cub whined in his sleep, and she was distracted by the sound. It was not normal for any of the people in her clan to have animals hanging around – the wild animals were hunted for food and wolves were usually killed if they came close to the clan members. Wolves were in direct competition with the clan for food and were known to attack people, especially small children. But she had become besotted with the cub in a very short space of time and smiled at him and looked back at Ranous and Rhidah who were also looking at the wolf cub. Geha picked up the plates from dinner to give scraps to Oonie. Rhidah cleared her throat and became flustered when she saw Geha looking at her. 'Thank you so much Geha, I have not had a cooked dinner since I was last together with my clan. It seems so very long ago.'

'Oh, that is terrible Rhidah. I guess Ea and Damika do not realise how disgusting the food is that they have for us – I remember it was like dried mush,' Ranous lamented. 'We had to put up with it for a short while and that was bad enough.' Geha smiled at the memory.

'You are right Ranous. I guess it was nutritious, but it tasted disgusting. I had forgotten how good real food tasted,' Rhidah responded. 'I am so pleased to be here. Though I do miss my clan and Veran …' She broke off no longer able to talk. She put her face down in her hands and started crying, overwhelmed by the memories.

Tears in his own eyes, Ranous shuffled over to Rhidah to cuddle her, and Geha gave a small whimper and slid downwards into the circle of arms also holding Rhidah close as she sobbed her anguish at the loss of her loved ones. Geha called on the spirits to cherish them as they all cried together, each for their own reasons. They sat there for some time comforting each other. The stars were shining, and the cooking fire was low when they decided it was time to go to bed. Geha shuffled to break free of the comforting arms and bumped into something furry near her side. Oonie had pulled the leash away from the bush and was drawn to the comfort of warm bodies. He was sitting close to Geha and did not bolt when she moved away from the other two. He looked up to her with trusting eyes. Ranous looked over at Oonie commenting, 'Here is another one who is smitten with you and your cooking Geha.' Ranous started laughing and Oonie cocked his head on one side and looked quizzically at him not sure whether to bolt or just stay close to Geha. Rhidah smiled for the first time in weeks.

Geha helped Rhidah to a bed in the cave while Ranous struggled to the bed where he and Geha had been sleeping. Geha administered some pain medication to both Rhidah and Ranous. Rhidah soon settled to sleep. Geha rolled exhausted into bed beside Ranous. He rolled over and gathered Geha in his arms and made love to her as silently as possible, not wanting to wake Rhidah. Oonie was happy to be close to his human friends and settled on the floor between the beds. All four slept soundly that night.

Chapter 17

Flying low over the parched red land revealed a vast emptiness. The drought was stretching further to the south. Ea and Damika scanned the horizon looking for drought-stricken animals to rescue for their latest project. They slowed the ship and flew sedately along the muddy remnants of a river. After a short while they found a group of wild sheep in a bog hole in the dried riverbed. Most of the sheep had died trying to get to the last of the green slimy water that was just out of reach of the dying animals. Two lambs and a ewe, however, were still alive – just. They had survived on the small puddle of polluted water that had welled up close to where they were stuck. They were looking quite emaciated and like the rest of the flock were stuck in the gooey mud.

They were so exhausted that they had given up struggling to get out of the mud and did not resist when Damika tied the rope around them and pulled them out of the sucking mud. Ea then hosed down the trio of woolly animals and they gave them some fresh water and grain. They eagerly drank and ate and quite exhausted they fell asleep under the shadow of Genesis. When they were dry the guardians levitated the sheep on board and flew off to drop them at Eden.

Damika could see that Geha and Ranous were expecting them. Oonie was threading himself around Geha's legs, obviously now very comfortable with his new home. He paused in mad excitement when the shadow of the ship hovered in the usual spot and the hatch opened. The cub all at once sprung to attention when Ea and Damika levitated themselves and the three sheep off Genesis. Geha quickly snatched up the cub before he tore over to investigate the sheep. Ea manoeuvered the ewe towards the grass next to the pool, and the lambs followed. The starving sheep did not need much herding as they could see and smell the luscious grass growing close by.

Ea said, 'We will need to go and cut some thorn bushes to create a temporary fence to keep the sheep safe.'

Damika returned to the ship and came back with a box of steel axes, knives and machetes. Geha had found the leash for Oonie and tied it to his collar. This sent him wriggling, squirming and whimpering trying to dislodge the rope around his neck. He was desperate to check out the sheep, which he was sure would taste great. Geha hung onto him and dragged him along behind her and tied him to a tree next to the pool. Ea, Damika, Geha and Ranous disappeared around behind the caves to an area where the thorn bushes grew. The four started enthusiastically cutting the bushes and stacking them for the trip back. Damika noticed that Ranous was doing more than his fair share of the work, and she was worried he would overdo it.

Rhidah appeared around the corner of the cave slowly hobbling on a crutch and sat down beside the wriggling cub and started rubbing his furry ears. Damika could see that it was an effort for her to move, and she was pleased Rhidah was trying to join in. Oonie loved the attention and cuddled up to Rhidah and fell asleep in the dappled sunlight dancing through the leaves of the tree where they were sitting.

After cutting a good amount of bush the four then dragged the pile back to the cave and they started making a fence from them around the front of a second cave. When they arrived back the three sheep were still gorging themselves on the lush grass. It took several trips before the fence was completed. Geha was tired, but Ranous was totally exhausted from his effort.

When the fence was completed, Rhidah let Oonie off his leash and he bounded over to the sheep trying to push through but eventually gave up. The thorn bush was too thick and spiky for him to push through. He squatted outside of the pen with his pink tongue lolling out of his mouth and he satisfied himself with watching the sheep very closely. After their initial scare the sheep ignored the cub and continued their feast. Geha laughed at the cub and said, 'I guess the sheep will be quite safe as long as Oonie can't get through the thorn bush.'

Damika said, 'The thorn bush is only a temporary fence. As soon as Ranous is well enough, we will show you how to build a permanent wooden fence. This will be quite necessary as we start increasing the flocks and herds. We will also be showing you how to plant wheat and barley and how to use it as a food. If we are going to set up a permanent spot to live in, it is going to be necessary to enable you to produce enough food to support whatever size group that will eventually be living here.'

'There are two more young people we will bring to this community soon,' Ea continued. 'Eden will grow and prosper. You three are the beginning of the new age.'

Geha, Ranous and Rhidah looked at each other suddenly aware how much work would be involved in building their community, but it was also very exciting.

Damika took a moment to examine Ranous's wound and was very happy with his progress. Geha looked at it before Damika bound it up again, and considering how hard he had worked that afternoon, she was surprised the wound was looking so healthy. Damika also examined Rhidah and was satisfied with her progress as well.

Ranous inquired, 'How soon will the others start arriving?'

Ea replied, 'As soon as we contact them. We will have to ensure a more permanent food source but until that happens, we can keep bringing in food from other places until you are self-sufficient as a community. There is enough space for all of you, but we will have to start building substantial shelter in time for the winter. The caves become quite damp during that time. Damika and I will be bringing in any younger animals that we find, but we will also need to start building fences to restrain the animals and keep them safe from Oonie and other wild animals. We will concentrate on sheep and goats first as they will reproduce much quicker than cattle. We will also bring in crops that we think will do well in this area. Do you have any more questions?'

'Yes,' replied Ranous, 'The axes, knives and machetes ... what are they made from? They are so much stronger than the stone axes we were using in the clan.'

Damika replied, 'They are made of stainless steel. You will have access to all the tools that you need for the jobs we have to do. It is now important that you get better as quickly as possible, and we will bring the other two people in to help with the building of this new community. When we have time, we will teach you the art of metallurgy. There are a lot of raw materials on this planet, and we can teach you to make your own metal tools.'

Ranous reached over to hold Geha's hand, and they looked at each other somewhat bewildered. The overload of information they had received in the past few days was overwhelming and they both had much to think about. Ea looked approvingly when Ranous pulled Geha protectively into his arms. Oonie sat beside Rhidah and licked her face. Rhidah pushed his mouth away but cuddled him for comfort.

'Ea and I are going now ... we will be back tomorrow,' Damika said. They walked back to the ship and sped off towards the east patrolling the planet.

Chapter 18

E a and Damika were now inspecting the lands that passed beneath them with more purpose than usual. They returned to the drought-stricken area where they picked up the sheep and started cruising along the river once more to find more livestock. On the horizon, however, they noticed a thick pall of black smoke that billowed into the sky.

'That does not look good – it is where Lomas and Keska's clan were last camped,' said Damika.

Ea said, 'Yes … it looks quite a large bushfire. The clan were camped by a large lagoon further up the river for their initiation ceremonies at the last full moon. With the drought I think they would still be close by, and they probably stayed in that area. All the wildlife will remain there for the same reason as this lagoon will not go dry as it is fed by springs from the artesian basin. I'll head straight for the lagoon.'

By this stage Genesis was travelling at maximum speed and the massive flames of the fire filled the view in front of them. The lagoon was between them and the fire and Ea suddenly decelerated as soon as they came close. Ea and Damika stared at the fire, mesmerised by the all-consuming inferno that confronted them and reflected in the water of the lagoon. Clouds of smoke then swirled between them and the fire which eclipsed their view. It was impossible to use their sensors to find the group of humans presumably still around the lagoon area. Occasional tongues of red and yellow flame thrust through the haze of smoke. A sudden gust of wind buffeted the ship and Damika lurched against the console. Ea steadied the ship as much as possible and dropped the ship almost level with the water. Even through the soundproof cabin, Ea and Damika heard the roar of the bushfire, and the two guardians were pleased to be separated from the fire by the incombustible hull of the ship. While they were aware of the massive flames consuming savannah in front of them, Ea and Damika were more concerned about Lomas and Keska and their clan. They crisscrossed the lagoon and its edges searching for people.

Sparks from the fire flew overhead and the tinder dry grass near the waterhole caught alight as the wind was providing oxygen to fuel the small advance fires. Damika noticed an animal bursting out of the smoke, its fur on fire, running for the safety of the lagoon. She ignored it and focused on scanning the area for the Lomas and Keska and their community.

'Over there Ea … I think I saw something in the water near the high bank in the middle,' said Damika.

Ea steered Genesis towards where Damika had indicated. Then he also saw where they were. The group had moved into the water under the overhang of a high cliff overlooking the water. They had brought their skins down with them to hide underneath as the fire passed around them. They had not heard the ship over the roar of the fire but now they had pulled the skins off their heads and were waving frantically at Genesis.

Ea wriggled the wings of the ship from side to side to indicate that they had seen the clan, but he was now alarmed as some of the people were leaving the relative safety of the water and trying to scramble out. He flew overhead and levitated fifteen of the clan on board the ship. He concentrated on selecting the younger ones who were shorter and who would be in danger of drowning and their mothers, and he included Lomas and Keska. Genesis did not have enough room for the remaining members of the community. The inferno was almost upon the group and there would not be time to take the first group to safety and then return for the rest. The community left behind realised what was happening and they returned to the relative safety of the water again to take their chances with the fire. As the flames moved closer to the bank the clan members saturated their skins and hid underneath the cover and waited for the fire to move on.

Ea gained altitude and rose over the top of the flames; the ship lurched violently from side to side as they moved through the centre of the fire. Damika raced to the embarkation room to check on the passengers who had been levitated into the ship. Lomas and Keska were there and a group of women and children. They looked wet, muddy and frantic, and the small children tried to hide behind their mothers' legs. They saw Damika come through the door and they gasped in trepidation. This was the first time they had seen the guardian up close and they threw themselves to the floor of the ship. Lomas and Keska smiled at Damika with relief and said, 'We are so pleased to see you and thank you for rescuing us and the others from the fire. We thought we were going to die.'

Damika looked at the two and sighed, 'No, at least you won't die but we could not pick up the entire group and we are not sure if they will survive.'

Lomas and Keska spoke to the others on board, helped the others upright and silenced their fears about Damika. The women were still worried, and the small children kept a watchful eye on the strange god and kept their distance, although not as panic stricken as before.

They looked out of the porthole of the ship as the smoke swirled, and the flames occasionally thrust red tongues of destruction through the chaos. They thought about the ones who were left behind in the water and prayed to the spirits for their survival. Ea circled the fire for some time until it had passed the waterhole and moved on. A change of wind direction moved the bushfire away from the rest of the lagoon.

Ea flew Genesis back to the lagoon and hovered above the area where they last saw the clan members. At the edge of the lagoon the remains of trees glowed, and ash powdered the ground around hot coals that still flamed and smoked angrily. In the water, to everyone's relief, they could see heads bobbing around. The remaining members of the clan had survived the fire. They stood up in the water and waved their saturated skins at Genesis. None of them appeared to have suffered any major problems – where they had chosen to ride out the fire was the safest place to be. The height of the bank ensured a distance between the fire and the water and the people in the water were safe. Those on board clapped and cheered, unable to believe that they had survived such a catastrophe.

Ea hovered the ship on the other side of the waterhole where the fire had not reached and waited for the rest of the community to swim to where they were. Ea, Damika and the others levitated to the ground and watched as the swimmers propelled themselves across the lagoon and helped each other out of the water. The clan members hugged each other, almost unable to believe they had survived.

Ea said, 'Well done everyone, it is amazing to see that all of you have survived such an event. The question now is where you will need to go. You can't stay here because it will take some time for the vegetation to grow and for the animals to come back. Everyone will starve unless we can move you to somewhere where the food is more plentiful.'

Damika said, 'What about the plains to the west of here, it is the same river but there have been good rains there in the last couple of months and the grass should be growing well, and the animals will be migrating to that area.'

Ea said, 'Good, we will start moving the group now.'

Damika enlisted Lomas and Keska to arrange clan members into groups and organise some people to pack up the camp gear where it had been left in the water. Within the space of a few hours the clan was reestablished in their new location. Ea had checked to make sure that no other clans were within the area to ensure the safety of these people.

On the final trip the only ones on the ship were Lomas, Keska and two of the warriors with the rest of the weapons and other tools necessary for the survival of the clan. Ea took a longer route back to the new location and they found a herd of cattle grazing on the grass growing on the plateau to the west of the river. The warriors looked out of the front of Genesis and started discussion about bringing a hunting party back there to catch cattle for food for the clan. Damika said, 'We could stampede a couple of them over the edge of the plateau to give the clan quick access to food right now – otherwise they could face being hungry waiting for the hunters to get the animals.'

'Indeed, a good idea Damika,' responded Ea and he flew the ship up over the edge of the plateau to where the cattle were grazing. He chose a couple of beasts, that were grazing close to the edge of the plateau and zoomed up behind them hitting the siren on board some distance from the cattle. All the cattle came alive at the sound and quickly picked up their heads and looked towards the sound. Ea also activated the flashing lights at the front of the ship. He now had the undivided attention of the cattle, that were now thoroughly stirred up, snorting and pawing at the ground, not sure of what this new threat was. Ea gave a second blast of the siren, and the cattle tuned tail and bolted towards the edge of the plateau.

'Oh no!' yelled Ea, 'I didn't want the whole lot over the edge. Just a couple would do fine.' He did some fancy mustering techniques with the ship, deftly slicing the herd in two and turning most of them away from the edge at the last moment. He spun the ship around just in time to see three cattle disappearing over the edge of plateau falling on the rocks below.

'Unbelievable!' exclaimed Lomas. 'That is a fantastic idea. I wouldn't be surprised that we will use that idea from now on.'

'That is good,' said Ea, 'But I hope they only take what they need. If they run the whole herd off the cliff, they won't be able to eat the lot and the whole herd will perish for no good reason. I think that we will pick up a couple of the young heifers to start off our herd back at Eden. But we will go and fetch the people from your clan to come and butcher the carcasses and return them to their new camp.'

Ea flew Genesis back to the new campsite and gathered people, tools and baskets to pick up the carcasses and return the meat to the campsite. Damika asked Lomas and Keska to remain behind on Genesis after this task was finished. Ea once more turned Genesis back towards the now thoroughly stirred up cattle and deliberately looked for young cattle who did not seem to be so disturbed by the recent crisis that the herd had endured. He flew over the top of five young heifers and levitated them into the hold. Damika raced down to the hold and misted the sedative on the heifers to stop a wild rampage in the ship. Keska and Lomas followed her to the hold and Keska said, 'OK, tell us what is going on?'

Damika replied, 'Let's go back to the cockpit and we can have a discussion of what is happening.' On the flight to Eden, Ea and Damika outlined the project that was happening at Eden, and Lomas and Keska were intrigued by the concept and agreed to meet the others. They also had Ea and Damika promise to return them to the clan if they did not want to stay at Eden. Ea levitated the heifers onto the grasslands on the other side of the pool and then flew the short distance to Eden.

Chapter 19

Genesis hovered in its usual spot near the cave and Oonie moaned a greeting to Ea and Damika. Ranous heard the familiar sound and burst out of the cave excited about the new arrivals, not sure if they were to be animals or humans. The hatch slid open, and Lomas and Keska emerged from the ship with Ea and Damika following them.

Ranous, knowing this was the beginning of something very special, felt his heartbeat increase, and he held his breath watching the newcomers, wondering how they would fit in with himself, Geha and Rhidah. Oonie, feeling some of the worry about the newcomers, hid behind Geha's legs and peered out at the two new people. Geha, Ranous and Rhidah had discussed this situation at length over the past few days, and it seemed so easy back then. Ranous kept walking towards Genesis not realising that Geha had slowed down. Damika introduced Lomas and Keska to Ranous. He rushed forward and hugged Lomas doing the manly thing in punching Lomas playfully on his arm pleased to see another man. He then turned to Keska to greet her with a hug as well. He suddenly realised that Geha was not with him, and he spun around and yelled, 'Come on Geha and say hello to the new members of our community.'

Keska kept walking down the path looking at Geha as she walked. Geha swallowed her fear and started moving towards Keska, a small uncertain smile starting on her face. 'Hi, I'm Geha ... you are welcome to our home,' said Geha formally.

'Hi, I'm Keska. Thank you for your offer,' she replied, just a little uncomfortable. Geha felt ashamed of her fear and held out her arms to hug Keska. They felt an instant connection with the physical touch. Oonie now more trusting of the others came out from behind Geha's legs and sniffed at Keska ready to disappear at the first sign of trouble. Keska was somewhat hesitant about the little wolf but turned the back of her hand for Oonie to smell and he tentatively licked her. She dropped down to the ground and hugged him, and he quickly decided that Keska was a friend and started jumping all over her. Ranous then introduced Oonie to Lomas and they were equally excited about meeting each other. Rhidah walked around the corner of the cave and then Geha introduced her to Lomas and Keska. Rhidah said, 'I have food back at the cave. Please come and have something to eat.'

Ea and Damika looked at each other and breathed a sigh of relief. 'So far so good,' Ea said. 'Let's get the pens built now.' Damika called to the others before they disappeared, 'Have something to eat and then come back to the sheep pens and help us make the permanent fences.'

Rhidah shyly shared some of the dried fruit she had been making following instructions from Damika. It tasted absolutely delicious, and Keska and Lomas asked how it was done. 'Damika has been showing us how to do it,' replied Rhidah, 'and we have been experimenting with all of the varieties of fruit growing here so we will have fruit to eat all year around – not just during the growing season.'

Geha and Ranous then showed the two around the cave, all of them talking excitedly. Oonie joined in with the fun and then it was time to check the outside.

Ea called them as they emerged into the sunlight. Ea and Damika had already cut and levitated logs from the forest to the site near the sheep pens and they were looking for more help as they wanted to teach the five the technique of cutting timber and making a basic fence to keep the livestock protected from predators – and Oonie. Ranous observed how Ea and Damika used lasers to cut the timber into planks, and they distributed saws and other hand tools to the four and showed them how to shape the rails to dovetail neatly with the posts.

Rhidah sat by the pool with Oonie and watched the others but kept bringing water and snacks for the workers, making sure they were well hydrated during the building of the fence. By the end of the day, they had finished enough pens for the sheep and a few spare pens for any other suitable livestock that Ea and Damika might find for the community. Ea and Damika walked the five over to where the cattle were grazing on the other side of the creek that was fed from the pool. Lomas and Keska then related the story about how they had been saved from the bushfire by Ea. The guardians then left to check what was happening on the rest of the planet.

Ranous showed Lomas and Keska their fish trap although it had no fish in it. They would eat some of the variety of food Rhidah had gathered during the day. They cooked the food together over the coals and relaxed talking about all they had done during the day. Keska noticed the waterfowl paddling amongst the reeds on the far side of the pool and said, 'We have slingshots to hunt water birds, and they are very tasty to eat.' She cut an appropriate twig on a tree with the machete and quickly fashioned a slingshot from fibres from the belt she was wearing. Keska then waded quietly into the pool and tracked the waterfowl through the reeds. The others watched fascinated by Keska's hunting skills. Lomas just smiled watching the scene he had seen so often in the past, proud of being able to show the others a skill they did not know. Keska quietly rose above the reeds, just high enough to find the waterfowl and quickly use the slingshot to fire a small rock towards the unsuspecting bird, knocking it unconscious. The rest of the terrified fowl lifted into the sky in a splatter of water and noise. Keska waded over to the bird lying limply on the water and picked it up and squelched her way back through the pool towards the others. Back at the table Keska showed the others how to prepare the fowl for eating and everyone was impressed with her knowledge and keen to learn another way of how to be self-sufficient. Lomas and Keska agreed to stay for longer than they initially agreed to.

Chapter 20

The personal early warning system started beeping an urgent warning. Ea looked at the warning beacon on his wrist, turned on his heel and sprinted back to the ship. The unrefined uranium would have to wait. The situation might be serious. Ea had a small supply of refined uranium on standby for such emergencies. Hopefully there would be enough to keep the energy banks full enough to withstand whatever the threat was that was facing them now. He sprinted around the corner of the rock wall that hid Genesis from view and noticed that the hatch was already open. He thought that was a bit strange, but he called out to Damika as he leapt through the opening. Damika turned around to see him entering the ship. The five young people who were with her also jumped up with surprise and Oonie started barking madly. Geha quickly shushed him into silence.

The computer screen glowed behind them. Ea suddenly forgot how urgent the warning was and stared at the group in front of him in the control room. It did not take him long to realise that Damika had been teaching the young people far more than they had agreed on. The books on the table showed the old writing script. Paper and pencils were scattered on the table in front of them.

In the silence, Ea's personal warning system started beeping more urgently and he turned to the control panel to find that the main warning system had been turned off by Damika. As Ea turned to the control panel, Oonie and the five quietly disembarked, knowing that Ea was angry with Damika and maybe them. Ea turned on his heel and moved to the control centre, turned on the warning system and checked what the external threat was. There, on the surveillance system, were signs that a fleet of ships was making its way through the far edges of the solar system.

Ea and Damika looked at each other, and the realisation occurred to both at the same time – the Chosen Ones had finally arrived after so many millennia. Ea and Damika had waited so long for them to arrive. Damika yelled, 'They're here … they are finally here.' She jumped up and down with excitement.

Ea touched Damika near her energy centre with his open hand. He even momentarily forgave her for teaching the children the ancient script. The five youth, still under the ship were confused by the excitement shown by the guardians but decided that they would make their way back to Eden via the path over the hill – Eden was a few hours walk from the uranium mine. Ea and Damika did not even notice they had gone.

Ea moved over to the computer and fed calculations into it to estimate how long it would be before the fleet arrived. The computer quickly returned the estimated time of arrival of the fleet at six months. Ea almost smiled and showed the calculations to Damika. She seemed disappointed that the arrival would still be so far away. Then she smiled and said, 'So it is finally happening.'

They no longer had the responsibility of stewardship of the planet. It had been quite a task for them to maintain the welfare of the plants, animals and humans in the New World, and in six months it would be all over. The alarm continued to beep urgently. Ea moved back over to the control panel and switched the noise off, while they continued their planning. Even androids had their limitations. The sound had been turned off, but the warning light was still mutely blinking its frantic alarm.

Chapter 21

'Well! That was interesting,' said Ranous as he grabbed his backpack and started to walk up the track towards Eden.

'What do you think happened?' said Keska. 'You know more about the guardians Geha, what do you think was happening?'

Ranous turned to watch Geha help Rhidah over some rocks. She said, 'Damika was certainly excited, but the only time they talked about the Chosen Ones was the first time they told us about the history of the Old World during our first meeting. Ea never gets excited, but he was definitely distracted. He didn't even comment on Damika teaching us the old script.'

Rhidah leant against a tree and took a sip out of her water container. 'I was on the ship for quite some time when I was recovering and I occasionally heard them talking about the Old World and the Chosen Ones. Ea was mostly talking about why it was important to collect us together and ensure our survival as we were the only ones left. Maybe we aren't the only ones left. I didn't know what they were talking about but maybe their reaction has something to do with the Chosen Ones arriving.'

Ranous turned and walked up the path, taking it slowly as Rhidah was still not completely recovered. Lomas was second in line to Ranous, and they jostled each other to be the first on the path, slashing at the undergrowth on each side with the machetes making the path more accessible for Geha and Keska to help Rhidah. Oonie was threading his way between each of his pack, wildly excited about the unexpected walk.

Ranous watched as Oonie ran ahead and he snuffed all the exotic smells of the bush and the trees and flushed out birds from the undergrowth. Then he disappeared as he dashed through the bushes, occasionally he gave small yips of excitement. Then trees and bush thrashed wildly. Oonie barked and growled, and the squealing of an enraged pig pointed to where an epic battle proceeded just out of sight. Ranous spun around towards the sound and grasped his machete more tightly, his battle instincts rising. Oonie suddenly yelped loudly, bolted out of the bush with blood streaming down his shoulder from an ugly gash. He instinctively darted towards Geha and held up his injured leg. The pig burst out of the bush behind him, its thick black mane bristled on its back. It squealed furiously, murder in its eyes as it searched for the wolf cub. Ranous reacted quickly and brought the machete down, hacking at the animal intent on killing their little wolf baby. Lomas yelled and joined in the battle. The pig, which had been focused on murdering the wolf, reassessed the situation and realised that even though it was greatly outnumbered, began to fight the two humans. Ranous thrust the machete into the pig and danced around it as it kept throwing its massive head from side-to-side and slashed at them with its razor-sharp tusks, all the time it squealed its murderous intent until its massive body slumped forwards, its lifeblood oozed away into the ground.

Ranous inhaled deep breaths, his shoulders tight and he poked the pig with the machete to make sure it was dead. Lomas walked over to Ranous and remarked at how much better the machetes were at dispatching an adversary than a wooden spear. Ranous, remembering the outcome of the bear hunt nodded in agreement.

Oonie pressed himself into Geha, as he whimpered and pleaded for help with his beautiful brown eyes. Geha quickly gathered some nearby vegetation to provide first aid to the little cub and checked the two men to make sure they were uninjured.

Ranous, finally getting his breath back, said, 'Lomas and I will stay behind to skin and dress the carcass of the pig and prepare it to take it back to Eden. We are not going to let this unexpected bonus of meat go to waste.'

Geha responded, 'We will go back to Eden with Oonie and get some baskets to bring the flesh back to Eden.'

Ranous watched Geha for a short while as she carried Oonie along the path and Keska helped Rhidah. Then he squatted down and helped Lomas to skin the pig carcass and cut it into chunks to take back to Eden.

Chapter 22

Geha carried Oonie back to Eden to stitch his wounds and give him some antibiotics from the supply that Damika had left at Eden. Rhidah stayed behind at Eden to look after Oonie and prepare for drying the pig flesh. With only five people to feed (and a hungry wolf) there was no way they could eat the meat before it went off, but Damika had shown them how to make jerky over hot coals and a drying rack. Rhidah sharpened the knives and collected wood to prepare the fire pits for the drying process.

Geha looked back at the campsite worried that Oonie would try to follow her, but he was sore, and his little body needed to rest, and he was happy to remain at Eden with Rhidah.

Geha and Keska were able to return to the battle site much quicker and were back at the site within a few hours.

The four did not talk much as they were all aware they were running out of time to return to Eden with their cargo of pig meat. Even though they were from different clans, the butchering of the meat went easily, and Geha reflected that other than the slingshot technology there was not much difference in the ways that she and Ranous prepared a carcass for travel back to the clan hearth compared to Lomas and Keska. It was dusk and they would be travelling through the night back to Eden.

Geha was the last to leave and she was giving thanks to the gods for the gift of food when she heard the snuffling of small animals close by. She finished her prayers and silently tracked the sounds to a small clearing near a pond. There was a small group of piglets snuffling and playing with each other. No wonder the sow fought so hard – this litter were her babies, and she was trying to protect them. Geha hurried after the others and shared her information about the piglets.

Chapter 23

'Trapping the piglets is one way of getting us to become more self-sufficient,' argued Lomas. 'They are quite small now so they may become prey to some predators without their mum to protect them. They will be easier to trap while they are little, and we have spare pens and can keep them safe. We just need to work out a way of trapping them.'

'Mmmm,' agreed Ranous, 'it was certainly a good idea … Oonie get out of the food.' Ranous spun around to push Oonie away from the remains of dinner. 'So much information is happening. I think this is a great idea – we can increase our livestock numbers. What does everyone think? Ea and Damika seem to be a bit distracted now and this is one way we can be proactive without relying on the guardians all the time.'

'I hope this doesn't mean that Damika is not going to continue to teach us … the elders of our clan taught us some good information about how to survive but the information from Damika has revealed all sorts of possibilities – agriculture, writing, pottery, metal tools … it all seems so possible and so impossible," Geha said. 'It seems now as if it will never happen that we might have to wait until the Chosen Ones arrive.'

'I know what you mean,' replied Rhidah, 'but it won't all happen straight away. I think it just happens one step at a time, and I think that my small step is to get some of the yams growing wild here down near where the piglets were, and I will bring them back to Eden for planting. We don't have any of those here. That is a good start.'

Ranous leaned over and kissed Geha on the top of her head and he folded her in his arms, hugging her. Over the top of her head, he saw Oonie stealing the last of the roasted pig meat off the stones leaving the pieces of vegetable for the rest of the group. No one had seen Oonie do it as they were all in deep discussion about the future of Eden. Ranous just smiled and let the cub go with his stash. His shoulder must be still sore from the pig bite, although it was now over a week since it happened, and he seemed much better. Ranous thought it was fair compensation since if it wasn't for Oonie they wouldn't have the pig meat to eat.

The vote from the group was that they would go hunting for the piglets and a plan was made about how to trap them. They decided to return to the site of Oonie's great battle the next morning.

Chapter 24

They woke at dawn and packed what was deemed necessary for the hunt including rope, nets, knives, axes, machetes, spears, dried food, canteens of water and their skins if they needed to camp. All six, including Oonie, were soon on their way. Oonie was still sore, but it would have been impossible to leave him at Eden on his own. They let the sheep out of the pens to graze on their own. They checked the cattle on the way and were satisfied with their progress in becoming tame as they were not worried about the humans and even the wolf cub walking past. Oonie was too small to be of any threat to the cattle although he liked to go with his human pack to check on them each day.

The group of enthusiastic walkers pushed through the dew-laden grass and walked towards the morning sun, which was slowly gathering strength and warmed the countryside around them. Autumn was on its way and there was a nip in the air. Ranous remembered they would have to ask the guardians about making permanent housing at Eden before winter and the rain set in. Wisps of fog still blanketed the low-lying ground, and yellow butterflies were flying around the small purple flowers that grew amongst the grass. Oonie thoroughly checked the area for dangerous beasts, like dragonflies and grasshoppers, and snapped at the small black bees flying at nose height.

After they had walked for an hour, the grasslands gave way to the rolling hills, and the sun was now quite warm. The small black flies swarmed around their faces and drank their sweat, each person constantly swatted ineffectively at the menace. Soon the trees grew much more densely as they hiked upwards, now making the journey much more pleasant. They had to follow a game trail along the edge of the stream as occasional outcrops of rocks and thick undergrowth made the path much more difficult to negotiate. The group eventually plopped down under a large tree beside a large pool of water and rested. They ate some dried fruit, nuts and strips of pork jerky. Oonie decided to spread himself out beside Geha and he fell asleep, worn out by the morning's activity. Oonie occasionally twitched in his sleep dreaming of the next chase making the others laugh.

Ranous heard rustling and snuffling on the other side of the water hole. He didn't shift his body but shifted his gaze to where the noise was coming from. A large black pig was coming down a path on the opposite side of the pool, followed by ten small piglets that emerged from the bracken. Ranous held his breath knowing that it was only a matter of time before Oonie would awaken and give chase. Even after his battle with the sow the previous week, Ranous thought that Oonie would be in the thick of it and would not have learned any lessons about how dangerous it was to fight pigs. He carefully looked around to see where he had left his spear and machete. He mimicked a familiar bird call and caught the attention of others and pointed at the sow. Each member of the group quietly grabbed their nearest weapon and watched the troop that wandered in for a drink. Some sixth sense awakened Oonie and he looked at Geha and stretched luxuriously. The sow started at the movement, and the small piglets scattered squealing shrilly back into the undergrowth. Oonie became a coiled string and like a flash of lightning leapt quickly to his feet and dashed over the shallow water and charged towards the pig. The sow snorted and focused her beady eyes on Oonie, stained tusks protruding above her snout.

Ranous groaned and looked behind him. He saw that each of the group was on high alert. A shiver of fear ran through his spine. Oonie growled again and faced off with the sow. Ranous jumped to his feet, grasped the machete and dashed towards the anticipated melee. Out of the corner of his eye Ranous saw the others also rise to their feet, weapons grasped in their hands. For the first time the sow realised that there was more than the wolf threatening her brood. Her head moved to take in the others, but she braced herself to attack Oonie as he was the closest opponent. Oonie charged across the last of the water and started to snap at the sow. She turned towards the wolf and engaged him in battle. Geha screamed as the pig stormed towards Oonie, terrified that it would slice her beloved pet with the deadly tusks. A caldron of wolf and pig swirled around the pool. Blood mixed freely with the muddy water from the gashes on both animals. Geha, worried that her little wolf buddy was being hurt again screamed at the pig and started waving her machete and ran towards the chaos.

Ranous could see as Geha sprinted towards the fight and he yelled, 'Stay away Geha, the pig will kill you!!' He gripped his weapon tighter and charged through the water towards the two animals. The pig saw Ranous stampeding towards her, and she suddenly tossed Oonie to one side and she faced Ranous, implicitly knowing he was far more dangerous than the wolf. The pig accelerated across the pool churning the mud and rushed to meet the man head on. Oonie feeling somewhat cheated, turned around and grabbed a mouthful of flesh on the flanks of the pig and hung on for dear life, hampering the progress of the pig that rushed towards Ranous. The pig, desperately trying to ignore the wolf, continued across the pool charging at the man. As Ranous lunged across the water his memories were of the bear and his adrenaline levels surged. He started screaming a battle cry. The pig redoubled her efforts to dislodge Oonie, shaking herself as she crashed through the middle of the pool to attack the man as the wolf clung on like a leech.

Ranous stopped and braced himself for the impact, machete in kill position. His hands were quite steady, having been in this position before. He deliberately slowed his breathing and focused intently on the pig. He knew he was not really in any danger as he could hear the others rushing towards the fight. The pig lunged towards the man, and they met in mortal combat. Ranous braced his machete as the sow powered towards him, and he aimed it towards her broad chest. Unaware of the danger, the sow opened her huge jaws ready to slice Ranous in two and he almost faltered, but he sucked in more air and gripped his machete tighter. The sow leapt into the air in full attack mode and landed on the machete which sliced her throat, severing the carotid artery which killed her almost instantly. She crashed into the water, her lifeblood spurted out of the gash, limbs twitched spasmodically. Geha and Lomas rushed to Ranous's side, with their weapons ready but soon realised that they were not needed. Oonie finally spat out the mouthful of pig and splashed his way over to Ranous, panting heavily and he jumped up putting his wet paws on Ranous's chest, looking up into his face seeking approval.

'Good boy Oonie ... good boy,' said Ranous as he vigorously scruffed the little wolf. 'I wish you were on the bear hunt Oonie.'

Geha came close to the two favourite objects of her life and hugged them closely, her heart still beating wildly. She then released them and closely examined them, expected them to be bleeding to death. Oonie had suffered some superficial gashes but seemed to be in no imminent danger like his last encounter, and it appeared the blood on Ranous was pig blood – and a lot of it.

Ranous, ever practical, then examined the body of the pig and picked up his machete and said, 'Well I guess we had better skin it and hang it – then we can dry some of the meat … I hope no one is sick of pig meat yet.' He laughed a little shakily – a post battle shudder running through him. Lomas brought a rope from their supplies and he and Ranous dragged the carcass back to dry ground and dragged the body of the pig up over a branch of a sturdy tree and gutted and skinned the pig. Leaving the body overnight to set the flesh.

Ranous gave a speech to the bravest hunter of the group and remarked that Oonie's first fight and his injury did not stop him from showing such courage in his second hunt. The group had a great lunch, feasting on the roasted offal of the pig. Oonie got the tastiest bits as he was voted the best hunter by five votes to nil. Geha was happy that the unexpected hunt did not result in any major injury to any of the group.

'It seems that this is an area with lots of pigs,' said Keska. 'Is there any point to capturing the piglets for domestication if it is so easy to hunt the wild pigs?'

The group thought about that for a few minutes and Lomas replied, 'It is a lot less risky if we domesticate them – we have had two hunts and Oonie was hurt in the first hunt remember. There are only five of us and we don't have the safety of a large clan to help us. We do have the guardians, and the Chosen Ones are on their way, but we don't know how many of them are in the fleet. What if we must teach them how to survive on this planet? I vote that we continue with our plan and re-evaluate when the Chosen Ones arrive.'

The other four thought for a moment and agreed with Lomas. Ranous said, 'Great idea Lomas, I think we should continue with the plan we had begun with the guardians. The sheep and cattle had been easy to domesticate, hopefully the piglets would be easy too.'

After lunch everyone in the group was busy with the slicing of the offal into thin strips and drying the pieces over the drying rack. Rhidah sat beside the fire patiently turning the meat into jerky. Oonie had spent the morning cleaning up the bits of the meat and catching up on his sleep. They set up camp for the night as they would need to cut up the carcass to take back to Eden the next day and work out when would be the best time to return to capture the piglets. There were now two groups of piglets to catch.

Oonie woke abruptly and went rigid. He gazed at the undergrowth on the opposite side of the pool. The ten piglets moved down the path towards the pool and made small snuffling noises. Oonie went to charge towards them, but Ranous grabbed the scruff of his neck and pulled him back. The little piglets seemed lost, not knowing where to go and what to do. They wandered down through the bracken to the pool and threw themselves into the water, slurping noisily. Oonie whined and it was enough to scare the piglets. Once again, they ran squealing noisily back into the undergrowth.

Lomas said, 'We need to get over to the other side of the pool and set up an ambush for the piglets. It is obvious they are thirsty, and they will return. I think this is their place to drink and they are used to coming here.'

Geha agreed with Lomas and said, 'Good idea. Let's get the nets and ropes and wait over the other side. There is still time today to catch them.'

Everyone collected nets, ropes and some weapons just in case there were other older pigs that came for a drink and would also be prepared for a fight. They quietly skirted the outside of the lagoon and found the track that the pigs had been using for access to the pool. Oonie was allowed to come but only under Geha's control. She was able to distract him with tidbits of fresh meat. They all took places on either side of the track and quietly settled down to see if the piglets returned. Within half an hour the piglets trotted down the track, obviously thirsty but not having a mother to check and warn them of any threats.

The humans and the wolf all watched from their vantage point above the path, Geha held onto Oonie, hand clamped around his snout, while the thirsty piglets trotted past them on the path to the pool. Ranous waited until the piglets were drinking and gave the signal. The six hunters then leapt down the bank and tore after the piglets. The piglets heard them coming and ran squealing, scattering over rocks, around trees and through bushes. Oonie was hot on the heels of one piglet ducking and diving through the undergrowth squealing loudly. He dived on the piglet grasping it around the leg. The piglet increased its level of screaming, pawing at the air. Ranous came crashing through the bush and threw himself on Oonie and the piglet, forcing Oonie's jaws apart to drop it. Blood was dripping from the piglet. Geha also came crashing through the bushes and examined the piglet as best she could while it was still wriggling and squealing and shoved it into a net. Ranous left Geha with the piglet, and he took off with Oonie to catch more. Two of the piglets took off over the pool and were attempting to swim away from their attackers. Lomas and Keska were the ones who were given the job of catching any of these piglets escaping over the water as they would be easy to catch in deeper water. Two more decided to escape back along the track and ran straight into nets strung across their path by the humans and were quickly caught. Rhidah was able to secure these piglets and roll them into nets awaiting the others to arrive to help her with the catch.

Geha yelled out, 'I'm over here!' and she heard Lomas and Keska pushing through the bushes, each with a screeching piglet in a net bag. Geha was securing the struggling piglet with a rope tied to a tree. Lomas and Keska shoved their piglets into a net and then attached them to a tree leaving the piglets thrashing and protesting loudly.

The three then went racing back through the undergrowth towards where they could hear Oonie and Ranous with another captured piglet. They followed the wild barking and squealing pig sound and within minutes they were all together, breathing heavily and laughing exuberantly, excited about the morning's work, having captured six of the ten piglets quite quickly. How exciting. Lomas and Keska grabbed the two piglets in the net along the path where Rhidah was set up. They were all sweating with exertion, while Geha was panting quite hard not understanding why she was not able to run as hard as she usually could and feeling a little nauseous with the exertion. It was taking quite a while for her to recover, and she had to sit down to recuperate. Ranous grabbed the spare net from her hand and stuck the still squealing piglet into it. After a short rest they all started breathing normally and noticed that they all had nasty scratches on each other's arms and legs from running through the thorn bushes. Oonie sat watching the piglet trying to tear its way out of the net. They wandered back to camp with the piglets in the bags and left them in the nets that were attached to ropes but able to access grass and bracken to hide in. After half an hour they were still unsettled and trying to escape the nets they were in.

'They aren't going to be squealing for the whole night, are they?' complained Ranous, 'We might as well take them back to Eden now if that is the case.'

'I'm too exhausted to do that,' said Geha. 'I will definitely sleep through any noise of these animals.'

'How are we going to capture the rest of them?' asked Lomas. He drank deeply from his water canteen and sat on the grassy section near the lagoon and sighed deeply. 'They would have bolted into their hideout, and I haven't got a clue where they might be, and they will be easy prey for predators.'

'We haven't forgotten our tracking skills from the clan, and I would back Oonie's skills as a tracker as well,' said Ranous. 'Let's see if we can track them and if we haven't found them by late this afternoon, we will just take what we have back to Eden in the morning.'

Rhidah stayed behind to continue to work on the jerky and keep an eye on the bags of piglets. Geha took the lead on tracking the remaining four piglets. They backtracked the little hoof prints from where they first saw them that morning. It wasn't difficult to track them as their prints were quite visible along the path in the soft dirt between the rocks. It was mid-afternoon before they tracked them up to a small dead-end valley thick with trees and dense undergrowth with a steep narrow rock-strewn path running down the middle of it. It was hard going for all of them except Oonie who did not even notice the hard climb. His pink tongue lolled out of his mouth when he periodically stopped and waited for his human pack to catch up. The piglets had bolted a long way from their usual hiding place.

At the end of the valley, they came onto a narrow-rugged granite entryway. As they pushed their way through, they found a small canyon with tall trees and thick bush behind. They could hear a waterfall that was running gently into a small pool at the back of the canyon. If the group had not been so focused on catching the piglets, they could not have failed to see the rugged beauty.

Oonie caught the scent of the piglets and rushed off up a small game path after them. They were caught in an area where there was only one way out and that was the way they had come in. Geha elected to stay at the entry to the small canyon as it appeared the four escapees were cornered. It would be so easy to catch these little guys. Ranous, Lomas, Keska and Oonie tore through the bush once more rounding up the squealing piglets. Ranous threw himself on one and it started squealing and kicking him in the stomach trying to get away. He rolled over holding the piglet up in the air as he rushed down to where Geha was blocking the entry to the canyon and gave her a quick kiss before handing over the screaming piglet to be put into a net. Lomas came tearing down to where Geha was with the next one but stopped to help Geha as she was still struggling with the first one. A tremendous squealing came from behind a tangled thicket of trees, which indicated that Oonie had caught his very own piglet and Ranous bolted over to where the noise was coming from and rescued the piglet from Oonie. He raced back with the piglet with Oonie snapping at the air, quite upset that Ranous had stolen his piglet. Keska and Lomas had cornered the last piglet, which was caught in some of the undergrowth and making a huge amount of noise and struggling to get out. They threw themselves towards the thrashing banshee and struggled to untangle it. Unbelievably the piglet then wriggled clear of the undergrowth and went screaming up over the bank of the canyon like a mountain goat and disappeared from their sight. Lomas gave up the chase and leaned against one of the trees. 'That's the last we will see of that one,' he gasped quite out of breath. Keska laughed and agreed. They both started back towards where Geha, Ranous and Oonie were dealing with the other three piglets.

They saw Genesis as it hummed overhead and they watched as the piglet was levitated into the belly of the ship. It then banked and headed back towards the campsite they had set up at the lagoon. 'Well … we could have asked Ea and Damika to catch them for us and saved a lot of time,' said Lomas.

'But we had so much fun,' protested Ranous, 'and I think it is good that we are contributing to our own progress.'

By the time the group had returned to the campsite, Ea and Damika had loaded the piglets from the morning's work and were waiting for the final three piglets so they could take them all back to

Eden. Ea and Damika gave the five the option to return to Eden on Genesis with the piglets, but they voted to stay at the lagoon overnight and return with the baskets of pig meat in the morning.

Geha watched Genesis flying away towards Eden with their cargo and then she walked back towards the lagoon, stripped off her tunic and stepped into the water. She luxuriously floated around and watched the clouds scudding overhead. The rest of them joined her in the lagoon splashing each other and having fun after their busy day. Oonie joined in with his people and paddled from one to the other enjoying the pats and the rubs. Eventually they took time to clean themselves thoroughly, and Geha checked their cuts and abrasions and applied some of her soothing salve, making sure to check Oonie as well. They then relaxed under the trees around the lagoon and ate a selection of fruits, nuts and fresh roasted meat. They animatedly discussed the thrilling hunt and talked excitedly about the future in such a beautiful place until the warmth of the day and the earlier exercise caused all of them to roll themselves into their skins and fall into a deep sleep on the grass under the large tree.

Chapter 25

Oonie started barking at Ea and Damika announcing that the group had arrived back at Eden. Ea and Damika were still at Eden and had started building the communal house for the group's winter quarters. Ranous smiled as he dropped his load onto the table at the front of the cave. Oonie rushed around and checked everything, especially the ten piglets in their new pen. Ea had returned the sheep to their pen when the early warning system alerted him the group was almost home. Oonie now divided his time between the two pens, shoving his nose through the slats of each pen. The sheep ignored him completely, but the piglets squealed their disapproval and fled to the back of the pen, rushing to get away from their nemesis. Oonie, happy to be home, crouched down under a tree and surveyed everything from a distance but never took his eyes off all that was happening.

Ranous and Lomas went to help Ea and Damika with the cutting of the timber for the house and the three women started with the slicing up of the meat in preparation for drying the jerky. Oonie, being exhausted from the two days of full-on work decided to sleep for the afternoon, doing little more than what was necessary, occasionally bothered by a fly or a loud noise which momentarily woke him, but he rolled over and continued his deep slumber. By the end of the day, with the technology available, the slabs of timber for the lodge were cut and stacked, ready to be used to erect a community winter dwelling the next day.

Ea and Damika sat with the group over their dinner that night to bring them up to date with where the fleet of ships was in relation to the planet. 'It is curious that they have locked onto our locator beam here, but they are not communicating with us as yet,' Ea said. 'But we will need to prepare this community for the winter and so we will have to continue with building the lodge for your sleeping quarters and a storage house for storing food – enough for the winter. As you are no longer with a clan to ensure your safety, you can no longer move to new hunting areas when food becomes scarce. We will always ensure you have enough food but if anything goes wrong you will need to have food in storage. The biggest need now is to grow and preserve fruit and vegetables. After we build the permanent huts, we will show you how to make pottery storage jars to store food that will make it safe from pests. I know you also want to learn metallurgy and how to make steel tools and how to mend the tools that break. When the Chosen Ones arrive in five months' time, it might change but you will be instrumental in showing them how to use the resources on this planet that they will not be aware of. We will be able to show them where the mineral resources are that can be used to power the building of the villages. We will have to relocate to the big river near the Sphinx as it will be more suitable for building villages and can be set up for irrigation of crops and domestication of animals to become a much larger self-supporting community. For the moment you will remain here for the winter, but we will move you over to the new area in spring when the Chosen Ones arrive. It has been thousands of years since Damika and I left the Old World and I have no idea how ideas and people have changed in this time frame. We can only assume their values are the same as when we left. We will remain as support for them and you, but I would assume they will take a leadership role on how everything will be managed after they arrive. Until they communicate with us, we have no idea how many people are on the ships and how they will manage everything. We need to be prepared for maybe 200 people and have enough food and shelter for them. So, for the next five months we need to work together to ensure all will be ready for them when they arrive.'

'Can you take us over to the new location so we can start planning for this move?' Geha asked.

'Yes, we were planning to do this after the construction of the buildings,' said Damika. 'It will be a good idea to get some sleep now and we can discuss this more tomorrow. You will think of more questions overnight, I am sure.'

Ea and Damika left to resume their guardianship of the planet. There was much discussion after they left and it was some time before the small community slept, despite the busy day.

Chapter 26

Over the following week, Eden was a hive of activity with Ea and Damika directing the erection of the waterproof and snug sleeping quarters and the pest-proof storage hut. There was a small celebration for the completion of the project, and afterwards everyone helped move the furniture out of the cave into the lodge. Oonie was in the way a lot and they tied him up under the tree to supervise the animals in the pens. By now the piglets had settled and were not as scared of Oonie and so the little community was at peace.

'When were you planning on taking us to see the new area?' asked Geha.

'The best time is now,' Damika replied. 'This project is finished. We can visit the area and still be back at Eden before sunset.'

Geha, Ranous, Lomas, Keska and Rhidah stood in the cockpit area of Genesis, watching the planet unfold under them as they flew. Oonie had been tied up in the ship's storage area as he could not be trusted to create some sort of foolishness. Ea was maintaining a proximity to the ground, so everyone could watch for suitable animals to collect for domestication on their way to the Sphinx. Lomas was the first to see the objects in the middle distance in front of the ship. A herd of horses thundered over the grassy woodlands. A magnificent black stallion was in full flight in front, with his harem streaming out behind him like the tail of a comet. Lomas pointed his finger at them and asked Ea to cruise over the top of the mob. He sucked in his breath and held it, the scene before him like pure poetry. All at once the stallion saw Genesis and he perceived danger for himself and his mares and slid to a halt. He faced Genesis pawing at the ground until the ship came too close and he rose into the air striking out with his hooves. The audience in the cockpit were fascinated by the incredible beauty and bravery of the stallion.

'I want him,' breathed Lomas, mesmerised by the steed. 'Think of how easy it would be to use horses to get around on.' Ea flew past the mob of horses but Lomas kept looking back at them until they were out of sight.

Ea continued towards the Sphinx. All but Lomas refocused on looking towards where Damika pointed. A large monument gradually filled the front screen of the ship. None of the young people had seen anything like it before. Ea cruised slowly past the monument that had the body of a lion and the face of a man with a headdress and the audience in the ship gazed with fascination at the structure. Ea continued along the massive river that revealed trees, grasslands and countless birds and wildlife.

Geha asked, 'Why did you not start our community here? There seems to be such a lot more resources here than at Eden?'

Damika replied, 'There are a lot more dangers here, and a community living here would need more people to ensure they are protected and able to carry out a larger building program, including an irrigation system and proper social order. At Eden it is safer with no predatory animals in the area, and it is much easier to support a smaller community there.'

Ea continued to fly around the area giving everyone a good look at the location and then hovered at the front of the Sphinx. They all levitated off the ship and Ea and Damika walked between the paws of the lion and opened a door to the interior of the monument. The five young people were curious about what was behind the doors and followed Ea and Damika inside. Lights went on and the five were astounded by the vastness of the room that was lined with metal cupboards with writing on them. With the rudimentary understanding of the old script that Damika had been teaching them, Geha could read some of the signs on the doors. General Knowledge, Philosophy and Psychology, Religion, Social Sciences, Languages ... so many more – and she wanted to know more, but Ea and Damika continued to walk towards the back of the room. Geha followed the rest of them, and they came to a set of polished steps cut into the rock. Beautiful murals were painted directly onto the walls of the corridor. Damika said, 'These are images of the Old World and Ea and I decided to print these on the walls as a reminder of the way it used to be.' The lights illuminated all the wonders as they walked along, and Lomas pointed out images of horses working closely with the people. Geha glanced at the others, and they were obviously as astonished as she was with all they were seeing. Oonie, unusually obedient, did not leave Geha's side. Ea pressed some buttons on a panel at the back of the room that looked like polished rock, and the panel became doors that silently slid open and revealed more wonders – machinery, tools and many things that Geha could not even imagine what they might have been used for. Ea started speaking; 'This monument houses all that remains of the Old World. It holds all the knowledge and resources needed to start a new society. When the Chosen Ones arrive in just over four months, they can make use of this and hopefully whatever they bring in their own ships will supplement this for the start of our new society. We have decided to show you this today to give you a taste of what the Old World had and what the New World could become. We are not going to stay today but we will bring you back closer to the time when the fleet will arrive.'

On the way back Geha had to smile when Lomas asked Ea to fly over where the horses were again. Geha was now intrigued also by the possibilities of the addition of horsepower to the community.

At dinner that night, Geha felt queasy and had to remove herself from the table to vomit her dinner. 'It must be all the excitement that is happening at the moment,' said Geha when she returned to the worried people in front of her.

'Are you having a baby?' asked Rhidah. 'Some of the clan women were sick when they were pregnant.'

Geha thought for a moment and tried to remember the last time she had a period. In all the excitement of the past few months she had forgotten. She looked at Ranous and he looked at her. Geha said, 'I think we will ask Damika in the morning when she arrives.' All discussion about the new location now finished and Rhidah, Lomas and Keska were all talking about a possible baby. Ranous grabbed Geha's hand, and they let the others talk but Geha and Ranous let the discussion wash over them, quite overwhelmed by the possibility of being parents.

Chapter 27

The six residents emerged from their new quarters the next morning and organised breakfast together at the fire pit in the kitchen area. The conversations turned to the two most important topics. While they were eating, the familiar shape came to a stop overhead and Damika emerged from the ship with a ewe, two more lambs and a ram to boost their sheep population. All six of them hurried up to Genesis to help put them in the pen with the other sheep. The ram became immediately interested in the ewe who bolted to the back of the pen with the two lambs. The new ewe and her two lambs bolted to the other side of the pen. The five young people observed the new additions. Oonie also showed a lot of interest in the newest arrivals and watched them through the slats of the fence with great interest. Geha patted his head to reassure him they were part of the community. She felt squirming in her tummy and hoped she was going to keep her breakfast down.

Ea said, 'These animals come from different flocks so it should be OK for at least the first generation of lambs to be fathered by the ram. We will gather more animals as required to increase the herds after we get better access to grazing land near the Sphinx. After the animals have tamed down maybe some of you can take them out to the grasslands area here to graze and take the pressure off the grass area here. But there are more important needs here today. We won't worry about wheat and other grains yet, but you will need to learn how to make pottery jars for the storage of grains, vegetables and fruit to protect your food from pests. Maybe Oonie will be valuable to rid you of rats and mice. Today we will go to a spot a short way from here to get some good quality clay to make some pots and then we will build a kiln to fire them. We will make a better kiln at the river when the Chosen Ones arrive but until then you can start on learning how to make them.'

'What is the wheat used for?' asked Rhidah.

'Wheat and other grains were very useful in the Old World,' Ea replied. 'It was ground down into flour and then they made bread and many tasty food items. We have been growing some of the wild grains near the Sphinx and experimenting with the best grains to use for that location. Some of it can be used for food and some needs to be kept for next year's planting. I can't wait for the Chosen Ones to arrive and see if it is of the same quality compared to the wheat from the Old World.'

'If you have some wheat, is it possible for us to try making some bread now?' asked Rhidah.

'Yes, that is a good idea,' said Ea. 'Damika and I can find some ripe seed and show you how to grind it and how to make yeast to make the bread – we have recipes for both. Today's job is to find some clay and show everyone how to make storage jars.'

'Great,' said Ranous, 'it sounds amazing. Let's go ... where is the clay? What does it look like?'

Damika led the way behind the waterfall and walked back along the creek bed that followed the stream back to the source. They followed her in a single file hiking along a game path, jumping from rock to rock, circling around thorn bushes and pulling up at the base of a cliff where there was another waterfall. Geha was feeling quite ill and had to sit down and then she started to vomit. Ranous stopped and sat with her. Damika walked back down the path and squatted beside Geha. She felt her head and checked her pulse. Ranous said, 'We think Geha might be having a baby. We remember some of the women back in our old clan seemed to get ill like this when they were having a baby.'

Damika said, 'Oh yes, this does happen. When we get back to Eden, I will give you a thorough examination back on Genesis and we will know for sure if you are. Are you OK to go on now?'

Geha indicated with a nod of her head that she was ready to go, and even though her guts were queasy, she didn't want to miss out on learning new information. Ranous helped her over the last bit of the path, and they walked towards the bottom of the cliff face and sat watching while Ea dug the dry clay at the edges of the pool. He showed the young people how to identify the best clay, and he pulled out sieves from his kit and showed them how to sift the chunks of clay into powder. They then gathered some powder into baskets and hauled it down the hill back to Eden.

Damika took Geha's hand and led her to Genesis. Ranous followed and Geha smiled at him. She was feeling nervous and very unsure of herself. She wondered why she felt this way as she was often in charge of the toddlers and children back with their clan. Geha felt stronger with Ranous being there with her and they followed Damika to the hospital section of Genesis. Geha remembered when Damika was saving Ranous from the spear wound. It seemed like a lifetime ago, but she worked it out in her mind that it was only half a year ago. Ranous helped her onto the bed and Damika started scanning her tummy for evidence of a new life. Damika pointed out where the baby was lying, and they heard the heartbeat – the sound of the first member of their new world. Geha was quite overwhelmed, and she started crying. Ranous held her, and he also cried. She smiled through her tears and thought about how she was now fully invested in the best possible start to their new life. How different would life have been if she had stayed with the clan and married Charthon. She involuntarily shivered and clasped hold of Ranous's hand much tighter. Ranous dried his tears, and he said, 'Well I guess we should go and share the good news with all the others.'

Ranous, Geha and Damika levitated to the ground, and Ranous, with his hand still holding Geha's, thrust their hands together into the air and let out a battle cry. Geha certainly wasn't prepared for that, and she spun around, totally surprised at his reaction before laughing. Rhidah, Lomas and Keska, who waited for the news nearby, also laughed and cheered. Ea looked up from where he kneaded wet clay on the pottery table. Oonie bounded over from his duty at the sheep pen, eager to join in the joyous occasion, jumping up around everyone receiving lots of rubs and vigorous pats. This was definitely a time for celebration.

Geha had a huge smile on her face. 'Yes, we are having a baby and Damika has given me some medicine to help with the nausea, but I am also going to look for some plants that Erua used for the women in the clan. I think I would like something to eat please.' The excited group scattered around and collected food for their celebratory lunch, and the guardians left and promised to be back the next day. Keska went to catch some quail near the reeds on the other side of the pool, as she knew that Geha loved the taste of quail. Lomas went to check the fish trap; Ranous found some bird's eggs and visited their beehive and collected some honey. Rhidah and Geha went to the small garden for vegetables and collected a variety of fruit for their celebration dinner. Back in the kitchen Geha boiled some water in preparation for cooking the quail. She and Rhidah were organising the food they had gathered from the garden. Rhidah also tasted the cordial she had made from fruit from the apricots and gave a nod of approval. For the first time in weeks Geha's mouth watered, imagining the taste of her favourite foods. She sent thanks to the gods for this wonderful future for her and her loved ones. Life was getting better and better.

Geha saw Keska coming back from her hunting trip, having caught the quail with her slingshot. She had already wrung their necks, and they had bled out as she walked back to the kitchen. Keska dunked the quail into the boiling water and plucked the feathers from their bodies, putting the feathers to the side in a bowl to use as decorations in their huts. They gutted the bodies and gave the offal to Oonie who was waiting patiently for his share of the bounty. Lomas came in and contributed to the feast with two large bream he found in the nets. Oonie had a second feast of fish guts and then decided to return to his guard duty at the sheep pen.

Dinner that night was a happy time for all, the celebration of so much to be grateful for and they all gave thanks to the gods as they had been taught.

Chapter 28

Lomas had been looking for an opening in the conversation to bring up the idea of having horses at Eden, and he started the discussion of the subject with a great deal of excitement. 'Ever since we saw the horses, I have been thinking about how useful they would be for getting from one place to another and they could be used for transporting stuff such as the clay yesterday. It could all be put into baskets and the horses could haul anything up and down from the river or anywhere. I saw images on the walls of the Sphinx with people from the Old World using horses – we could do the same, especially if we could make some carts with wheels. It would make it so much quicker. What do you think Ea? Is that a good idea?'

Ea was in the middle of showing Lomas, Keska and Rhidah how to make clay pots for storing food. They paused with what they were doing and all looked up at Ea for his thoughts. Ea thought about it for a few moments. 'I'm not so sure that it would be so easy to domesticate the horses. You saw how wild the stallion was.' he said. 'I will do some research on horses being used for transport as I believe that horses need to be broken in to accept being used for riding and to pull carts. It is not the same as domesticating the sheep and the pigs for food.'

'All of the other animals have settled down quite well here so far. Could we please just try?' Lomas pleaded.

Keska put the finishing touches on her jar and swirled some little patterns around it, making it quite unique. She seemed to have a talent for making pots. 'Perhaps we could bring some of the younger horses here and see how easily they can be tamed,' she said. 'That stallion was so magnificent, and it would be a shame to see him confined to a pen.'

'Can they be put out to the pasture with the cattle?' asked Ranous.

'I remember that a lot of livestock in the Old World were pastured together, and I don't think they attacked each other. They are herbivores – they won't attack each other,' responded Ea. 'I guess they can be eaten like the other hoofed animals, but I do agree their usefulness as transport would far outweigh their usefulness as food.'

Damika returned from where she, Ranous and Geha had finished construction of the kiln for firing the pots that the others had made. 'We need to collect some suitable wood for firing the pots,' she said and looked at the pots that the others had made. Damika was quite impressed. 'This is what you can all be making when winter comes. Also, something else you can do during the winter is to knit and weave the wool from the sheep and make it into warm clothing and blankets. The wool can be shorn from the sheep soon in preparation for the winter chores. There is so much to learn. But we have a lot of time, and when the Chosen Ones arrive, I think they will be happy to teach you all that is necessary for beginning a new society.' Keska and Rhidah showed Geha and Ranous how to make clay pots and the discussion about the horses was forgotten for the rest of the day.

Chapter 29

Damika deftly touched the controls and cruised over the hills where they had been only days ago. The black stallion cantered over the grasslands with his harem, and Ea reflected on his conversation with Lomas.

'Do you think it is a good idea for us to bring some horses to Eden?' Ea asked.

'Horses?' asked Damika. 'How will they help the group? Would they be used for food?'

'No,' said Ea. 'Lomas put forward a good proposal for them to be tamed and then used for transport for themselves and for carrying heavy loads like the clay.'

'OK, that sounds like a good idea,' Damika responded. 'How soon would they be able to organise somewhere to keep them?'

'Lomas suggested they could graze on the grassland area where the cattle are,' Ea said.

'Ahh! He was very sure of himself then,' said Damika. 'Shall we do it?'

'I think I will do some research into how difficult it will be to train a horse first,' he said and turned to the computer for information about horses. He soon looked up from his search and said, 'We can give it a try – at the very worst the horses can become food.'

Damika stopped her meandering over the surface of the planet and returned to the area with the horses. She handed the controls over to Ea and they flew low over the herd and selected a mare with a filly foal and the stallion. She misted some sedative over the stallion and levitated him into the belly of the ship. She also misted a sedative over the mare and foal, and they were also levitated into the ship. Aware of the need for speed, Ea increased velocity and zoomed up above the surface of the Earth to get to Eden as quickly as possible with their cargo.

Within hours they were back at Eden and the three horses were levitated onto the grass, several kilometres away from the cattle. Ea and Damika waited in the distance for the sedative to wear off watching them closely. As it wore off the horses did not show their usual spirit and dominance. They were disoriented and quite uneasy about the new space and shied away from objects that weren't familiar to them.

Ea said, 'I think we should go to get the young people and show them our newest addition.' He lifted Genesis into the air and flew a short distance to Eden.

Everyone met Genesis at the usual spot and demanded to know what was new. Ea said, 'We have selected three horses, and they are in the cow paddock.' Lomas let out a loud whoop and not even waiting for Genesis to load, took off over the stream to where the cow paddock was. Ranous took off after him, also excited about the horses.

The stallion was still half groggy and moving hesitantly, hanging his head and shaking it trying to clear the sedative from his brain.

Lomas leapt over a large fallen tree that was in the way and raced over to where the stallion was. He threw his arm around the horse's head. The stallion trembled with the unknown touch and whickered in fear. Lomas was delighted with the horse, rubbed him and continuously talked to him softly, knowing instinctively how to talk to him. The stallion continued to tremble, shaking his head to clear the fuzzy feeling. Lomas was also trembling with excitement, unable to believe that the magnificent animal was at Eden. He tried to reduce his excitement levels knowing it could frighten the horse even more. He continued to talk gently to the horse and rubbed him softly in long strokes down his neck and head. This course of action seemed to be working, and Ranous, who was watching from the fallen tree, started to relax.

The others arrived and they also watched Lomas from the safety of the tree. Even Ea and Damika were impressed with his seeming natural connection with the animal. Oonie had been watching the events with his face pushed between Geha's legs also watching, panting softly. The filly was taking much longer to recuperate from the sedative than the stallion, and she was still lying under a tree off to the side out of sight. Nobody was taking much notice of her, but Oonie was distracted by the filly when she started to move. Oonie quietly pulled his face away from Geha's legs and circled around the side of the tree instinctively tracking the filly. No one noticed as they all continued to watch Lomas and the stallion.

The filly was unaware that Oonie had come around behind her until Oonie gave her a nip on her leg. The filly started thrashing the ground trying to stand up and simultaneously take flight. The filly now somewhat awake but disorientated struck out at the unknown assailant screaming loudly and rearing with fright. Oonie, excited by the action, started barking furiously at the filly. The mare suddenly aware that her offspring was in danger, galloped over to where Oonie was barking at the filly.

The stallion, also now fully awake, reared up, spun around, and fully wild, unleashed all its fury. He lashed out, teeth bared, and kicked out at Lomas. A deadly hoof connected with Lomas's cheek, the loud crack audible to all the stunned audience. Oonie continued to bark and snap at the filly adding to the noise and confusion. The stallion trampled Lomas who was now on the ground unconscious. Keska screamed and ran towards Lomas. The stallion saw her and with murder in his eyes lunged towards Keska. Ranous pushed Geha back over the tree trunk, grabbed a hunk of dead tree branch and ran towards the stallion waving it to get the attention of the horse and refocus its attention away from Keska. Geha sprinted towards Oonie, calling him to leave the filly alone but he was having too much fun. The stallion spun away from Ranous and raced to protect his mare and foal, kicking out at Oonie when he came closer. The stallion then wheeled away and cantered off in the opposite direction and disappeared over the hill, the mare and foal swept along in his slipstream. Oonie pursued them, barking furiously. With the horses and wolf a distant echo, the silence was deafening. Keska bent over Lomas's still inert body, afraid to touch him. He had a huge bruise rapidly darkening on his cheekbone. Blood puddled out of his mouth and ran down the side of his face and neck. Geha gave up trying to call Oonie back and decided to check on Lomas, sending prayers to the spirits for his safe recovery. Ea had disappeared back to Genesis and Damika leaned over Lomas to check how badly hurt he was. It wasn't long before the shadow of Genesis hovered overhead. Slowly Lomas, Damika, Geha and Keska levitated into the ship. He was still alive – wonder of wonders. Keska breathed a sigh of relief and helped Damika move him to the hospital bed. Damika ran a full scan over his body to ascertain his injuries. 'He has a broken cheekbone, collarbone and arm, a dislocated knee and some broken teeth, bruising and concussion so he is very lucky. He is going to have a massive headache and be out of action for a few weeks, but I think that is about all,' Damika said. The others watched as Damika set his arm and knee and attended to his other injuries and gave him painkillers. Lomas regained consciousness gradually and he groaned when he saw his arm in a full splint. 'You are going to be sore for a few weeks, and I will fix your teeth in a few days when your cheekbone is less swollen,' Damika said.

When he was stabilised, Lomas was taken back to the lodge and Keska stayed with him. The rest of the group went and sat beside the pool area. 'And I thought the worst thing that could happen today would be the pots we made yesterday fell apart,' mused Geha.

Ranous returned from the cow paddock carrying a thoroughly unrepentant wolf. Oonie lapped water from the pool and plopped himself down under his favourite tree and observed everyone for a short while before he fell asleep, worn out from his morning's work.

'What is going to happen to the horses?' Geha asked Ea.

'We will find them with Genesis and return them to the herd,' replied Ea. 'I don't think there is any need to continue with the attempt to tame the older horses – our best outcome has been with the younger animals so far and I think we should continue with that idea for all animals we gather for our project.'

'I think it would be possible that they could be a good addition to our program,' Geha said, 'but I agree we need to get younger horses. Like the younger pigs and sheep, they will be able to be domesticated easier, and I agree with Lomas that when they are trained, they will make our lives easier.'

'Do you think we should recapture the filly and return her here then or should we just return her to the mob and capture younger foals?' asked Ea.

It seemed strange for the Ea to ask for advice, and Geha wasn't sure of the answer. 'Capture the filly first and see what condition she is in,' Geha replied.

'Do you want to come with us to find her?' Ea asked.

'Sounds good,' said Geha. 'I think we should keep them in a pen near the sheep to ensure they can observe us from a safe distance and maybe that will make them more responsive to taming.'

Geha, Ranous and Rhidah took to the air in Genesis and circled around the grassland area until they spotted the three horses casually munching grass close to some trees, seemingly unaffected by their close encounter with humans that morning. However, when they spotted Genesis overhead the horses reacted aggressively, the stallion now fully recovered, reared into the air striking out at the ship. Geha, Ranous and Rhidah watched the horses as they were sedated and levitated into the hold for the journey home.

'I am glad the stallion is returning to his home. This animal was not meant for domestication; he has a spirit that will never be broken. He would rather die than submit to being owned by a human,' Rhidah reflected.

Geha had to agree. 'This animal is meant to be free, and I am thinking that his herd will be happy to see him back.'

When they found the herd, Ea and Damika returned the three horses to a grove of trees not far from where the rest of the horses were grazing. They waited until they were back on their feet and started to walk around. Ea cruised the ship over the herd as they prepared to return to Eden. Ranous spotted a lame mare that struggled to keep up with the others and he pointed her out to Ea. 'That is a possible horse that would be perfect for our needs at Eden,' Ranous observed.

'She has a foal as well. We will need to find another colt from another herd sometime in the future for the best start to our horse's program.'

Ea smiled at Ranous's observation. These young people were very much in tune with the ability to work with the land and not for greed and pride. He thought that maybe on this planet and in this time, they might finally be able to achieve the plan that the Cognoscenti had as their vision for the future. He felt very comfortable with the project as it naturally unfolded with very little assistance.

Ea nodded and he cruised overhead so that Damika could administer the sedative on the two horses and levitate them into the hold. The return trip was happier than the trip to the herd. The three youth were checking the computer banks and soon making plans for the training of the horses. They all agreed Oonie would definitely be staying behind at the lodge when they worked with the horses, and for the moment the horses would be confined to a spare pen back at the cave area until they were completely tame. They could not risk any recurrence of what happened with the stallion.

While the mare was still sedated, Damika checked what her trouble was and started treatment on her hoof. 'If she is confined to the small pen, she should recover quite well,' said Damika. 'She had a small piece of wood under her hoof which was infected. I have removed it and given her antibiotics. We will keep an eye on it over the next few days and make sure she is okay.'

'Let's get her back to the pen and see how she settles over the next few days,' Ea said.

Ranous brought food for the mare and her foal, and they waited back under a tree some distance from the horses and observed them. The mare was apprehensive about being in a new place, but she showed interest in the food straight away and the little foal was happy to be with her mum. It was obvious that the selection of this mare and her foal was much more thoughtful than the other three.

Geha sent thanks to the great spirit for the gift of another two animals for this expanding community at Eden and for the good health of Lomas. Aside from the setbacks from the past week, things to be grateful for still outnumbered the difficulties.

Despite the mare being confined to a small pen, she seemed content. Oonie was not allowed anywhere near the pen until both the horses and the wolf were used to each other.

They wandered back to the lodge and checked on the pots that were drying in the sun. Damika went inside to check on Lomas to make sure he was as comfortable as he could be. Lomas was sitting up in bed and Keska was feeding him some soup that was about as good a meal he was going to get until his broken jaw and teeth were mended. He looked like a bruised mess, but he seemed comfortable enough and Damika was happy with his progress when she checked him. Lomas looked disappointed when Damika told him the stallion had been returned to his herd, but he did a lopsided smile when Damika shared news they had captured a mare and her foal that were currently in the spare pen.

Damika returned outside where the others were at the pottery table and watched as Ranous was grinding some of the broken pots back to fine clay. Oonie was tied up underneath the table and looking very sad. Now that they had a mare and foal in the pen close to the lodge, Oonie was not allowed to wander free. Damika said, 'Are you being a good boy Oonie?'

Oonie pricked up his ears when he heard his name mentioned but he just lay there with his paws covering his nose on the ground. Oonie swiveled his eyes around to see who was talking to him and his tail thumped the table leg, but he did not attempt to get up. He knew he was a bad boy.

Ea spoke to the three young people about the clay. 'Clay can be completely dried and broken down into powder again many times to make new pots. Each time you make these you are going to get better at doing them. It's just a matter of practice and if they are not of good enough quality, you can reuse the clay. Until the pots are fired you can reuse it a few more times.'

Rhidah and Geha were making new pots from the damp clay, and they were having fun making rings of clay and placing them on top of each other experimenting with building larger pots. They squeezed the rings together to make a solid wall on each of the pots trying to make sure the thickness of each wall was the same so the pots would dry evenly and not crack as they dried. Geha giggled and pulled off some clay to show Rhidah how to make a handle for the pot. She happily chatted while making her pot and cheered the others up with her frivolous conversation pulling all of them out of the doldrums and reminded them that they had so much to be grateful for.

Satisfied with their progress, the girls cleaned up their area and put the pots in the sun to dry. Geha suddenly felt a cold nose cautiously pushed into her hand. She smiled and looked down at an apologetic Oonie and said, 'Oonie, you have made some really bad choices this week, but I will teach you how to be an obedient little wolf in future. For the moment you will need to be on the leash while the horses are in the pen.' She gave Oonie a hug and he was overjoyed with her reaction, licked her hands and then reached up to her face for a lick. Geha pushed him away saying, 'You haven't been forgiven that much.' Oonie was happy to just be allowed back his with his favourite person and laid under the table and watched her constantly. Ranous, Geha and Rhidah worked together to prepare the evening meal for all of them, and Oonie quickly picked up the scraps that accidentally fell off the table. Keska ate with the others and returned with soup for Lomas to eat.

Chapter 30

A few days later Keska followed Lomas out of the lodge. The early morning sun felt so good, she felt like she had been away from the fresh air for days. Lomas hunched over, clearly still in some pain from his injuries. Damika had fixed his knee, but his broken arm and collarbone were still an issue. Damika had also said she could fix his teeth today as most of the swelling in his mouth had reduced to the point where she could operate on his mouth. He was still feeling sorry for himself, and he was sick of eating mush. Keska could see that Ranous, Geha and Rhidah were finishing their breakfast. Geha handed Lomas some painkillers and a cup of water. Keska followed Lomas and watched him sit down and then went to find something for their breakfast. Geha laughed. 'Come on ... it's so good to see you up and about Lomas. We need to make some more pots ... come on everyone, we need to do more work.' It was easier for the others to comply with her requests although they were all feeling rather lazy in the nice warm sun, but they all knew it was becoming colder and the last of autumn was gradually sliding into a cold and wet winter. The nomadic lifestyle and moving to a new place with warmer weather was no longer an option. They would have to make their little group more resilient and become capable of surviving the winter. Making storage pots was essential for their survival. They struggled to their feet groaning with effort and wandered off after her towards the kiln area. 'Come on and help us with the pots Keska, we are all nearly as good as you now in making them – we have had more practice,' laughed Geha.

Keska put a bowl of stewed fruit in front of Lomas and grabbed some jerky and nuts to eat on the short walk to the kiln. She replied, 'Yes, I'm coming, I need to get out and do something. Show me what you have all made. Are there enough good pots to be able to do a firing soon? This is going to be so great and I'm really looking forward to it.'

Rhidah laughed. 'There are enough down at the kiln for the first firing right now as we have been waiting for you to join us. We knew you would be disappointed if you missed it. This is what you are so good at Keska. We had to wait for you.'

Keska felt so much warmth for her friends and felt some tears of gratitude well in her eyes. She quickly wiped them away and followed the others. 'You are such good friends,' she said. 'Are we doing that now? I would really love that.'

They wandered down to where the kiln was ready for the first firing of pots. It was so exciting. Everyone gathered around handing the pots to Ranous and he loaded them the way Damika had showed them, stacking them so that none of the pots touched any other pot and enough space between them to allow the even baking of the pottery. Even Lomas with his bruised body and ego decided to join the others and he was infected by the joy of the others. The quietest member of the group was Oonie who was watching the group sadly, still attached to a bush by his lead while the others were having fun.

When they had finished setting the pots inside the kiln Geha said, 'Come on Keska you can light the fire.'

Keska felt honored that the others had chosen her to light the fire. Damika said it would take three days for the pots to be fired, and each member of the community would take turns to sit by the kiln, feeding the fire to ensure a constant temperature for three days. Keska felt so excited. This was her talent, and she wanted this project to succeed so badly. It was so important for their survival to be able to store their food.

For three days she fed the fire and barely slept. Lomas came to sit with her, and the others took turns to feed the fire to give her a break. By the third day the pots were ready, and the fire was allowed to go out. It took another two days for the pots to cool down and everyone was excited to see what they were like. Keska was so anxious and made sure everyone was waiting. 'Let's have a look and see what we have,' she said as she dramatically opened the kiln and held her breath, secretly worried about how many of the pots survived the firing process. Damika had warned them that a large percentage of pots would have flaws that would make the pot break in the firing process. The others sat around the kiln watching the pots as she handed them out. Keska carefully examined each pot and was relieved when most of them had survived the process. Everyone became increasingly excited about their success. They gathered up the pots and carried them up to the storage hut.

Ea and Damika arrived, and they viewed the pots. Damika said, 'This calls for a celebration everyone – this is another huge step in the direction of self-sufficiency.'

Geha laughed and said, 'Keska is the main reason this is so successful. She is so talented at making sure the clay is so well prepared that not many of the pots failed.'

'This was a team effort everyone, but we need to get back to making more pots tomorrow,' Keska said. Everyone groaned but laughed with her, knowing this had been far more successful than what was expected. When she went to sleep that night, Keska dreamed about making pots and woke up with many new ideas. The next day everyone threw themselves into making more pots, becoming more adventurous with their individual styles each trying to outdo Keska, but it was rare for this to happen.

Chapter 31

E a walked over to the breakfast table and casually asked who wanted to learn how to make cast bronze. After weeks of working on making pots, the young people looked at Ea with interest and jumped up from the table talking excitedly about this new craft. Ea took them down to the kiln area and showed them examples of bronze plough shares, sickles and tips for arrows and spears. The raw materials were in abundance near Eden and casting bronze implements was not much more difficult than making pottery. Ea showed them how to melt the ingots of tin and copper in a charcoal fire which was made extremely hot using bellows. Then using ceramic moulds, they poured the melted bronze to make items that would be useful for farming and protection. It was hard and hot work but very exciting. Ever since Ranous had seen the steel machete, he had wanted to learn the process of metallurgy and it was such an exhilarating time for him.

Lomas, still unable to physically help, watched for a while and then wandered off towards the pool. He caught sight of the two horses in the pen, and a light came back in his eyes. He turned towards the horse pen. The others noticed him moving over to the horses and all of them stopped to watch what he was doing. Keska stood frozen to the spot not sure of what would happen. No one had done anything with the horses other than feed and water them, content to just let them settle into their new surroundings.

Lomas started talking softly to the two horses and they looked around at him and nickered softly back at him. They turned away from him and started eating again. He quietly moved himself around outside of the pen, still talking softly to the two horses. They ignored him until he got too close and then they moved away. Lomas stayed where he was and kept talking to them. He relaxed and just leaned over the rail watching the mare and filly. He remembered the beautiful stallion and the complete waste of such a remarkable animal. Lomas turned around to the others who were watching him, and he smiled broadly at his family. Keska relaxed and smiled back at him, happy that he still showed the same deep curiosity and affection for the horses he had before the accident.

Chapter 32

Some days later Ea and Damika arrived at Eden and announced to all that it was time to go and harvest the wheat that Ea and Damika were experimenting with an hour's flying time to the north of Eden. They boarded the Genesis and took with them bronze sickles they had made the previous week and their baskets to collect the grain to thresh back at Eden to store for the winter.

Geha watched out of the porthole and saw the fields of ripe grain that waved in unison with the gentle wind as they flew over the top of the field and hovered off to the side. Geha sighed, this looked quite perfect. Damika called them together and showed them how to test that the grain was thoroughly ripe and how to harvest the ears. Geha let Oonie off his leash and this was the first time he was allowed to run free since the horse accident. He was in his element, enjoying every moment of this exciting day, chasing butterflies and bees. One of the bees eventually took offence at his close contact and stung him. He yelped in pain and bolted to Geha's side holding onto his sore muzzle with his paw. Geha had to feel sorry for her little wolf and gave him a cuddle, pulled out the sting and put some ointment on his muzzle from her kit of herbals. It didn't take long for him to be out again having fun, but he had learned to avoid the bees.

Damika allowed them to take a break in the middle of the day, and they wandered down near the small stream running at the edge of the field. They ate and filled their water canisters from the stream. Geha looked longingly at the stream and would have loved a swim and an afternoon siesta. She glanced around at everyone, and they all seemed as tired as her and she reflected that life in a settlement was so much more hard work than being in the clan.

Damika did not let them rest long and she kept them working hard all day. 'If it rains, we will lose the rest of the crop. The quality of the seed will deteriorate, and we need to harvest as much of it as possible before the rain begins,' she said.

Geha groaned and pulled herself up off the ground from where she was lying. The baby kicked viciously, obviously disturbed from its sleep. Geha rubbed her tummy and shushed the baby. She grabbed her basket ready for another stint in the field. What looked so pretty at the beginning of the day was now looking like a lot of hard work. Geha looked across at Lomas knowing that he was finding this work a challenge. His knee was healed but he was forcing himself to push through the pain by using medicine provided by Damika.

At the end of the day, they collected and loaded the grain into Genesis and returned to Eden. When they arrived, Damika instructed them how to lay the ears out on the blankets on the ground to allow them to dry some more. Damika warned them that the grain had to be perfectly dry to be able to be stored. If it was even a little moist the grain would become mouldy, and they would lose the whole pot of grain. Geha sighed – it was definitely more work than being in the clan.

The group ate quickly and slept soundly, being totally exhausted from the effort of the harvest. The next morning was the same. They all boarded the Genesis with their baskets and repeated the process of harvesting their crop. Geha looked around at the end of the day and saw that it would take another three days of hard work to harvest the rest of the ears. She looked to the west, half-hoping she could see rain clouds. No luck. It was such a pity this hard work had to be done by hand.

Wearily they emerged from Genesis for the second day carrying the baskets of ears. They carried them into the area where they were doing the drying and looked at the destruction on the blankets. Something had been in there while they were away and had eaten all the grains of wheat from the ears lying on the blankets. All that was left were the husks and straw. Unbelievable! Geha was devasted and she looked at the faces of the rest of her family. They all sat down heavily on the ground. All the hard work they had done yesterday was for nothing. Damika looked amongst the straw for evidence of what had eaten their harvest and found rat droppings amongst the straw.

'Rats ... dirty disgusting creatures,' she said with a lot of vehemence as she kicked the blanket, 'Now it is going to be difficult to keep them out of here as they know that you have food here.'

'We will have to leave someone here, or Oonie by himself to make sure that the rats don't eat any more of our wheat,' Geha said sadly. 'But what if he bothers the horses if he is off the leash?'

Lomas was still in quite a lot of pain from the accident and grabbed some more painkillers and a cup of water. Geha watched him and said, 'Lomas will have to stay to make sure the rats don't get to the grain. It is important for us to have everyone helping with the harvest, but there is no point with everyone working all day if the rats are going to eat everything while we are away, and we can't be sure that Oonie would not be distracted by the other animals in the pens outside. Rats are particularly cunning and would only come out if it was safe for them to do so. Lomas is still in considerable pain, and it makes sense he stay behind to guard the grain, and then he can also do other work here at the lodge while we are harvesting.'

Everyone agreed with Geha and Ranous grabbed the blankets and took the remains of the husks and straw over to the pens for the animals to share. When he brought the blanket back, they all despondently placed the ears of wheat they had harvested for the day onto the blankets.

They rolled the blankets that the grains were drying on to prevent dew from getting into the seeds and now added protection from rats and hoisted them from hooks on the ceiling in the storage shed. They then ate and wearily found their beds for a few hours' sleep until they returned to the harvest in the morning. Lomas remained behind and assumed guard duty over the grain sitting in the sun to dry.

The others grabbed their baskets and headed off to the Genesis. 'I hope bread is worth all of this work,' said Rhidah as they all tramped aboard.

They were old hands at harvesting the wheat by now and they good-naturedly threw themselves into their work, and they again went down to the stream during the middle of the day to have lunch. Oonie became somewhat bored after he got the scraps from everyone's lunch, and he went wandering down the stream in search of adventure.

Not too long after everyone could hear whining and high-pitched yipping from Oonie, quite unlike any other noises he usually made. Intrigued by the unusual noises being made by him, everyone jumped to their feet and raced to find what he was upset about. Geha was the first one to find Oonie and she started laughing at the funny sight that met her eyes. Oonie was bailed up by two small kittens which were hissing and spitting at him with all their might, their backs arched as high as they could go and standing side-on looking as ferocious as they could possibly get for their size. Ranous, Keska and Rhidah came scooting to a stop and they melted at the sight of the two small brown spotted kittens that were backed up against a crevice in a rock beside the stream. There were various 'ahhhs' and 'awwws' from all members of the group. 'OK Oonie, now you have found them, what are you going to do with them?' said Ranous. Oonie never shifted his gaze on the fierce little felines, and he started a high-pitched whine. Geha looked around the area wondering where the kittens' mother was. Further downstream she found the mum, dead with the body of a snake beside her. 'It seems the mum was protecting the kittens from a snake, and they are both dead down here,' she said.

Keska, getting as close to the kittens as she could, noticed they seemed very undernourished and probably starving. She raced back to where they had their lunch and found some leftover meat. She returned to where the kittens were and threw some of the scraps towards them. The kittens tried to resist the meat for some time, and the group withdrew from their spot, pulling on Oonie's collar to come with them. From the bushes a bit further back, they saw the kittens tentatively check the meat and then gulp it down hungrily. 'Poor little mites,' said Rhidah.

'Let's leave them there while we finish harvesting today,' said Rhidah, 'And then we can work out what to do with them later.'

'Well, they would solve our rat problem,' said Geha as they were walking back to the wheat field.

'Oh course,' said Keska. 'But how are we going to catch them?'

As they were harvesting the crop for the rest of the afternoon, they discussed the problem, and no one noticed Oonie was missing from the area. Ea and Damika could also see the benefits of taking the kittens back to Eden, and they gave suggestions for capturing the kittens. The afternoon's harvest went quickly, and they were all more excited about the harvest than they had been in the previous two days. At the end of the day, they realised as they put the baskets of wheat into the Genesis, that Oonie was nowhere to be found. Geha said, 'I will only give everyone one guess as to where he is.' They all started laughing and made their way downstream to find Oonie curled up near the rock with two kittens curled up beside him purring their little hearts out.

'OK so you worked out what to do with them I see Oonie,' remarked Ranous.

Geha had brought a basket and a cloth. Oonie stayed in one spot while Ranous and Geha reached over and grabbed the two kittens and shoved them in the basket and covered it over with the cloth. The kittens hissed and spat dramatically and were not at all happy with their change of environment. Ranous took the basket, holding the cloth closely over the top and Oonie walked beside the kittens, whimpering softly at the basket. The kittens settled down and they were transported back to Eden with the wheat.

Lomas was happy to see the rest of his friends and was fascinated by the two small kittens that hissed and fluffed their fur whenever the cover on the basket was raised. Ranous put the basket with the kittens in it in a quiet area of the storage shed and left some scraps of meat beside the basket for the hungry little babies.

They then left them alone and went to lay out the ears of wheat and get some food for themselves as well. The talk around the table that night was very animated, and a lot of laughter resounded around the lodge. Oonie was allowed to sleep with the kittens in the storage shed where the wheat was drying and all went to bed much more optimistic about the future than they had been the day before.

By the time the group had finished the harvesting a couple of days later the ears of wheat were ready for threshing and the kittens had totally integrated themselves with Oonie and the human members of the family. The kittens provided a lot of entertainment, and they showed their love to the members of their family by keeping the rodents away from the wheat.

It took the group a couple of days to thresh the wheat and stack it in the pottery jars. Damika kept some aside and showed them all how to grind the grain with a mortar and pestle to create flour. She then showed them how to make yeast and turn the flour into a flat bread and cooked it in a metal pan over the coals.

'A huge success Damika. I take it all back,' exclaimed Rhidah. 'This is absolutely delicious.'

The group sat back cooking more of the flat bread and topping it with meat or fruit, watching the rain tumble down outside. Oonie sat on Geha's feet and watched the two kittens as they took turns to check who had the softest lap. Having nothing else to do for the day, the stories of the newest members of the family started flowing freely and it seemed indeed that it was paradise on earth and life was good for this community.

Chapter 33

The lights on the console were now flashing continuously enough for Ea to stop and look. It had been several months since he had turned off the sound of the early warning system but now the increased flashing of the device made him curious about what was happening to the arrival of the Chosen Ones. The screen showed the relative distance of the fleet from the planet and Ea had estimated that it would take them roughly six months to reach their planet. They would still be about four weeks from their planet, but Ea suddenly felt the need to check on that progress.

Ea reached out and turned on the volume of the device to examine what update the computer was trying to tell him. Immediately the early warning system bleated its terrifying message. 'Unidentified craft flying in this solar system ... warning ... warning ... warning ... Unknown craft flying in this solar system ... warning ... warning ... warning.' Ea immediately consulted the computer for more information and checked the position of the craft and the size of the fleet moving towards the planet.

What he found chilled his sensors.

'Damika, you need to come here now,' yelled Ea. Damika came running from the hold of Genesis alarmed by the tone of Ea's voice. He gestured towards the console. She moved closer and listened to the deadly message and perused the information being relayed by the computer system.

'Oh no! It's not the Chosen Ones. Who could it be Ea?'

'Is it possible that it is the Tartarans?' said Ea. 'We never found out what happened to the Old World. It just seems too much of a coincidence that the Old World seems to have completely disappeared just after they connected with the Old World, and then we never heard from the Chosen Ones again. We have had the passive radar on since we arrived, sending out information about our position here. We need to turn that off immediately but I guess it is already too late.' Ea sent instructions to the computer and turned off the beam. Ea then sent messages to the database to search the memory banks for information about the Tartarans.

'It is still possible it is the Chosen Ones in different craft,' Damika said while they were waiting for the information to upload.

'Yes, that is possible,' replied Ea. 'But why haven't they sent out identification signals to warn us that it is them?'

Ea and Damika started reading the collective information on the database about the Tartarans and the news was not good.

'What can we do ... do you think if it is the Tartarans that they know we are here, and do they want to exterminate us like the Old World and why do they want to do that? What about our project ... how can we protect our planet?' said Damika with anguish evident in her voice.

'We need to plan,' said Ea, leaning over to read the computer screen. 'It appears the fleet will reach here in about five weeks ... we have that long to organise the safety of our community and whatever we need to do to save everyone and everything. Let's go to Eden and talk to the group there. They will need to know the full extent of the situation and they will need to work closely with us to find the best solution for the survival of the world.'

They flew to Eden and outlined the full extent of the crisis that had just unfolded. Previously Ea had given the group a sanitised version of their exit from the Old World and the colonisation of the New World. Ea spoke for a long time to tell the story about the history of the Old World and the Chosen Ones and their decision to send the guardians in Genesis with seeds and embryos of all living things from the Old World. He had previously told them about the seeding of the New World and the decision to implant the embryos into the clan people. Ea began the meeting lightheartedly, but the five young living there could sense something was not quite right. Even Oonie sat under the table with his nose over Geha's feet, resting quietly. Damika watched the faces of the young people seeing a gamut of feelings running across their faces … fear, despair, horror… and dead silence when Ea finished his story. Eventually Ranous asked, 'Why would the Tartarans hate humans so much to want to eradicate them from the universe?'

Ea sighed and elaborated, 'The Old World was originally colonised by the Tartarans many millennia ago. They are a group of humanoids who had super intelligence and were technologically superior, but they lacked the human capacity of emotions like love and empathy. History shows that they would come to a planet with the sole purpose of populating it and totally consuming the resources of the planet and then moving on to another. The hunt for resources to sustain their original planet and their ruling class was limitless. They maintained total control of all intelligent species on each planet and would enslave them until the resources were drained. They actively hunted down any resistance to their control and if they were particularly displeased with the residents, they would blow up the planet when they left. But they were more likely to leave a military force on the ravaged planet as an outstation for jump off points for further colonisation of other planets in their quest for domination of the known universe.

'It appears that after they had first occupied the Old World, for some reason they lost contact with the governing body of the Tartarans after a nuclear war early in the process which destroyed the main Tartaran city. This resulted in a loss of contact with the people of the central Tartaran government. Scout ships from the central government flew past but there was no response to signals, so the Tartarans did not even land on the planet to check it out. Those who survived the nuclear blast were plunged into a dark age and the records of Tartaran heritage were lost. After many generations they lost the knowledge of their purpose of existence. The survivors had no way of contacting the central government and so they had to rely on the humans of the Old World to survive. The Tartarans intermarried with the original people and descendants evolved with characteristics of both races. It seemed that the political and economic leaders of the Old World inherited the Tartaran characteristics, and they had a natural tendency to rule with no consideration for other people or the planet, and they seemed to be following their instincts of greed and malevolence even without the guidance of the central government of Tartarus. But some of the scientific community quietly became a part of the movement for protecting people and the environment, and they had a secret association with people who were like-minded. They initially tried to restore a small part of the planet but when they realised it had passed the point of no return, they diverted funding for our project to find a new planet and restart civilization with a different focus. When it appeared the community was no longer safe, the Chosen Ones sent us in Genesis with the seeds and embryos and promised to follow close behind. We have been waiting for the Chosen Ones to appear here ever since we arrived, and several months ago we assumed the fleet now arriving was bringing the Chosen Ones. It now appears it is the Tartarans who have been tracking us down, and as punishment they probably want to destroy the planet. We are not sure if they are aware that we have been here for some time or whether they have been tracking us from our passive tracking radar, but they are locked on course to our planet, and it appears they are still dedicated to the eradication of free-thinking human beings in their known universe.'

Geha's mouth was dry, and she could feel the familiar bile rising from her stomach. She wished it was just morning sickness. She felt the baby kicking and carefully folded her hands protectively around her stomach, feeling sick with the worry of what would happen to their near future. She now had so much to live for.

She looked across the table to where Ranous was and caught his eye. He also looked worried. When he saw Geha, he moved around the table and came to stand behind her. He put his arms around her and kissed the top of her head murmuring, 'It's OK … we will survive … trust me… we will survive.'

The tears started pouring down Geha's face and Ranous pulled her gently off the chair to hold her while she sobbed. Her heart was breaking and although she felt the love and presence from the others around her, she felt desperately unhappy – it just wasn't fair. She clung to Ranous like he was the only source of life. The rest of the community gathered around in a group hug. They were concerned because Geha was their leader, and they were somewhat lost without her usual calm response. Some of the others also started sobbing, now that it hit them their community might not survive after the next month. Oonie, never far from Geha started pawing at her with concern in his eyes, whimpering softly. Her heaving sobs came steadily. Ranous just cradled her until her the weeping reduced enough to be able to soothe her. Oonie pushed his way to the middle of the group and put his cold nose on her arm and tried to lick her face. Ranous did not even try to push him away. Eventually she started talking in between occasional sobs and hiccups. 'Why does this happen when we have all worked so hard to start this community. We have just started learning to write our language and metallurgy and pottery and our beautiful animals. What is this going to do to our life and to our world? We have only just started to learn about our parent world from the guardians … I have just started understanding about the reason for living and we are going to all die … it is so unfair … and the baby…. and Keska is now pregnant too.'

Ranous, knowing how to respond, continued to hold her and let her cry herself out, knowing that when she had finished crying, she would come up with some ideas of how they would all survive. That was the way she was, and Ranous knew her well enough to wait for her to reach that point. Oonie was also waiting for her to stop crying, his muzzle now resting on her leg and he constantly investigated her face waiting for that moment as well. He was puzzled by her deep distress but was reassured by the reaction of Ranous and so he made small whimpering noises willing to wait until his mistress was her usual happy self again.

Eventually Geha drew in a shuddering sigh and gave Ranous a kiss on the mouth and said, 'I love you so much, and I love the baby so much too and I love all of you so much. We need to work out a way that we can all survive. We don't have much time.' Geha gave Oonie a big pat and his pink tongue gave her cheek a swipe of approval, his world was back in order. He was ecstatic about that, and Ranous also was relieved that Geha had worked through her misery. Rhidah brought them back to reality by suggesting they have something to eat so they gathered back in the kitchen area, all working on something for a light supper with bread and leftovers. With the guardians still there, they talked late into the night talking strategy about where the best place would be to hide from the Tartarans and survive a possible major attack on the planet.

Geha mentioned that the cave system where they lived could be blocked up and they could all survive anything that happened. Ea and Damika, however, knew that the caves at Eden would not withstand an atomic blast which is what probably had happened in the Old World. The youth of the New World had no concept of the power of such a blast, but Ea was fully aware but did not believe until now that this could happen in the New World. But the idea did give Damika an idea of a set of caves in the mountains north of Eden. The caves were high enough in altitude to withstand anything except a direct bomb blast and any tsunamis. It also had a natural underground water supply and lower caverns that would be able to store food for an extended period. It had not been used as the original settlement for the community as it was a harsh and remote area – already there was snow on the mountains around there – not at all a paradise such as Eden. But it would be much safer from the Tartarans, and it was not far for the community to make their way back to Eden after the attack was over. It was the perfect place to hide the community for years unless the whole planet did not survive. In that eventuality the whole of their civilisation was in danger of extermination, but they had to at least try.

Geha asked, 'Is it possible for some of our extended clans to join us in the shelter.' She still remembered her friendship with Ouref and hoped that she would be able to offer sanctuary for her with their family. Ea replied that it was impossible for them to be able to ensure the survival of their own group. They would not be able to make a huge shelter with only five weeks until the Tartarans arrived, and they needed to make the shelter big enough for up to ten residents and basic needs for a year. Geha reluctantly agreed to the restrictions. 'Will you be sheltering with us then?' asked Geha.

Ea replied, 'No they will keep looking for evidence of human settlement, and if we are out there to respond to their attack they will know they have us and so we need to be out there when they arrive. We only have one ship with limited weapons, and they have a whole fleet. We have little chance of annihilating them, but we need to do as much damage as possible to the fleet. We have set up the Sphinx as the place for the Chosen Ones to find us but that will be obvious to the Tartarans and that will be the first place they will attack. We will need to move anything of importance to us away from there and put it in the caves where it will be hidden and safe.'

Chapter 34

The guardians loaded the young people on board Genesis, and they flew to the mountains to check how they could turn it into a secure area for the group and their animals, and store enough food for a year. The caves were hidden from the front, covered by trees and tumbled rocks. Ea led the way into the sinuous system that wound deeply into the subterranean caverns a long way underneath the entrance. The air was chilled but good quality even one kilometre underground. The quality of the water was excellent and would be enough for their needs. Ea used equipment to find a second entry to the cave system and plotted an area to get access to more oxygen with a filter to ensure clean air, even with a nuclear attack. They discussed what they would need for six months and started making plans for what they needed and what the priorities were. The difficulty would be enough food and wood for cooking while the crisis was happening. After finding the best cavern for their projected time underground, they returned to Eden to continue planning.

'What will happen to our own animals?' asked Geha. Ea indicated that the cattle, sheep and the horses could be left out in the paddock, and we can take the pigs back to the area where they captured them. After this is over you can go back to catch more, and the tame ones will probably be easy to capture again. There are not enough animals to reveal this area being a human settlement. I am thinking that the Tartarans will not recognise that Eden is an actual community. We will disguise the lodges, the kiln and stack the other equipment in the caves. The Tartarans will be looking over the whole planet for human settlement and if we can hide this tiny part of the world hopefully it will be undamaged, and you can return to Eden after they have finished with their destruction. You should all be able to return and continue with our project. We can assume that the Sphinx will be their first target and hopefully they will assume that all humans will be in the same area so they will heavily bombard that area and leave the rest of the planet alone. I think they will attack any of the clans who are out in the open, but we can't rescue them.'

Geha let the tears flow for her clan who would be in so much danger, but she knew her allegiance was with her own family now. Ranous rubbed her back and kissed the top of her head. Geha focused on her list of things that needed to be done and started organising jobs for each person that needed to be done to move food, wood and other essentials to the caves.

The first need was to make jerky to ensure protein levels. They also found other places in the world where cereal crops were growing wild and threshed rice, wheat, barley and corn and preserved the grain in ceramic pots. The five young people worked overtime to make pottery jars, and the kiln was working full-time. Fruit was collected from trees around the world, dried and preserved before being stored in pottery jars. Seeds were kept and stored in the jars. They then used Genesis to transport everything to the caves, including large amounts of firewood which was stacked in one of the large underground caverns.

While the young people slept, Ea and Damika removed the information and machines from the Sphinx and moved them to the cave system. Genesis was stripped of all useful equipment and placed in the caves. The community was going to have a great deal of time on their hands in the next few months, and they would be able to read and plan for when it was safe to emerge from their shelter.

Ea and Damika knew that their chance of survival against the Tartaran fleet was slim, and they prepared the community as well as they could for a future without them. They left computers for the community but without power they would be useless, and they had run out of time to teach them how to mine the uranium to power the machines. Ea now realised that Damika teaching them to read was the best idea, and that the five young people could access the information in the books. A simple mirror system was set up to feed sunlight down to the cavern where the young people were going to live so they would have light and vitamin D. Ea and Damika, knowing their own future could well be limited, kept checking the computer screen on the Genesis hoping for a miracle that the people of the Old World must have hoped for themselves so many millennia ago.

Chapter 35

With only hours before the Tartaran fleet was due; Ea and Damika had their last contact with the group. Geha and Rhidah organised their last dinner together at Eden before they flew them to the caves for the last time. Rhidah had outdone herself and despite the seriousness of the situation the five dined on the best food available to them at Eden. Geha raised a cup of juice to the family and to Ea and Damika who had made this all possible. 'To the future!' shouted Geha. The others raised their cups and drank to everyone's health and prosperity. Even the baby in her stomach joined the celebration and kicked joyously. Geha closed her eyes and sent a prayer to the gods who had never let her down. They cleaned up one last time and all were levitated into Genesis. The five humans, Oonie, Fluff and Max felt the nervous energy and could not settle. Ea dropped camouflage nets over the top of the now empty buildings and the kiln. Everyone looked out of the portholes of Genesis and watched Eden recede from view. Conversation was not required.

At the caves, the family disembarked quickly knowing time was running out. Ea and Damika checked to make sure that there was no sign of human activity in the area and gave a final dip of their wings to the community as they flew off for the most important task as the guardians of this small planet that they had called home for millennia. The first snowfall was lightly dusting the mountain covering any evidence of human activity as they lifted Genesis away from the mountain.

Ea and Damika reviewed the systems of the Genesis, knowing that they only had a limited amount of firepower and had to use all the chances they were given to save the world. They did not think of their own existence ... their sole purpose from the beginning was to populate the planet with the seeds and embryos of the Old World and to protect all of that from any harm. They were going to do that job to the best of their ability right to the end. Ea and Damika lay in wait for the fleet to arrive, planning to at least destroy the main Tartaran ship hoping that the rest of the fleet would then move away from the planet leaving it intact. They flew dark without any surveillance systems actively working – relying on their visuals to track the fleet. It was not difficult as the Tartaran fleet were not concerned about hiding themselves.

The fleet circled the planet looking for the humans who populated it and looking for weaknesses so they could blast it apart. Tracking the ships from a distance away, Ea and Damika watched the resplendent fleet of ships consisting of spaceships of similar shapes and except for the main ship, all the same size. The sun shone off the malignant metal surfaces of the craft making them highly visible to all residents of the planet. Ea and Damika surreptitiously followed the fleet, assessing their weaknesses and planned how they could inflict the maximum amount of damage on the Tartaran fleet and knew that they had to maximise every chance to destroy the main ship and as many of the others ships before they would become the target of the remainder of the fleet. They followed and witnessed them as they shredded the Sphinx into shrapnel – bits exploding into small projectiles of destruction. Two ships peeled off to land and explore what was left of what they thought was evidence of a human colony. Ea said, 'We could take this moment to take out these two ships right now – the others have left them behind.'

Damika replied, 'The rest of the fleet would know instantly what happened, and they will return and kill us, and we would probably not get the main ship in a full-on battle. We would lose the element of surprise.'

Hugging the landscape of the place that was so familiar to them, Ea followed the Tartaran fleet when they found a group of hunters and gatherers. A group of smaller ships peeled off from the main fleet and started a bombardment of the helpless community. Ammunition poured out of the ships and peppered the unfortunate clan people who fell to the ground powerless against the onslaught. They had no hope of surviving the firepower and Ea and Damika were relieved that their community was relatively safe in the caves They followed at a safe distance watching as the fleet indiscriminately strafed more innocent hunters and gatherers and started dropping more destructive weapons. White hot flashes of incendiaries incinerated the very air and flashed repeatedly across the sky like a demonic thunderstorm. Deadly winds thundered through the air tearing mountains apart, throwing particles of dirt and ash high into the atmosphere.

Geha and Ea watched as clan people, birds and animals were scorched and blinded by the deadly fire and they ran in fright, breathing heavily before succumbing to the fatal force. Fires raged through the forests, and it seemed as if the land itself was being torn asunder. Parts of the earth sank below the seas and flat lands rolled and heaved producing instant mountains.

It seemed as if the Tartarans had forgotten all else in their blood lust and Ea and Damika took the chance to inflict some damage on the main ship before they consumed the whole planet in their rage. Ea said, 'It is time – if we wait much longer there will be nothing left.' They followed the fleet to where it was night.

Damika loaded the largest nuclear weapon they had and waited for Ea to tell her to fire. Coming from behind the fleet they lined up the main ship and turned on their sensors to lock on their aim at the main ship.

'Fire!' yelled Ea.

Damika instantly punched the button, and the missile ran true on its path, streaking through the black sky exploding the main ship and the two others beside it, causing the three ships to vaporise in a flash of brilliant light. Ea threw a sharp U-turn and turned off the sensor again to outrun the rest of the ships that whirled around to attack their aggressor. Ea intensified the speed and pointed Genesis towards the canyon that he knew would hide them. Ea hugged the canyon wall and turned off the sensors that would give away their position. Damika reloaded their ammunition supply. The Tartaran ships all at once knew they had a fight on their hands and formed a defense shield and started tracking Genesis. The Tartaran ships sent out locator beams to find Genesis, now focused on finding them to exterminate the unexpected attacker. The ships spread out slowly moving over the surface of the planet in a grid pattern, checking the landscape with blazing search lights and locator beams. Ea and Damika watched from their position against the canyon wall as they passed by several kilometres to the south. Ea waited until they flew past and making sure that Damika was ready, they slowly tracked the fleet from the rear until they were ready to fire on some Tartaran ships that had bunched up close. Ea turned on the sensor again and aimed Genesis at the ships now in his sights.

'Fire!!!!' yelled Ea.

Damika slammed the button again and held onto the seat as Ea threw the ship into another violent U-turn. Ea turned off the sensors and used his knowledge of the planet to hide themselves from the Tartarans again. He was playing a cat and mouse game with the enemy, and he knew they would eventually run out of ammunition and luck, but if they could destroy as many of the Tartarans before they perished, they would have given the planet the best possible chance to survive. They ducked and weaved through familiar territory deliberately staying the dark side of the planet, making it more difficult for the Tartarans to find them. Ea headed towards another area where he knew they could hide and returned the ship to dark running mode. Damika loaded more missiles into the firing chamber and waited in the dark for the next moment in this battle. Ea called – 'They are coming in from the front.'

Damika groaned. She wondered if the Tartarans would see them as they passed over or whether Genesis was too well hidden to evade detection. Through the porthole she could see them coming – their search lights coming closer and closer. She watched the lights, wondering if Genesis was in the shadow area between the two ships now searching for them. She watched, waiting for orders from Ea and watching the ships slowly approaching. Ea, watching from the front, could see that the searchlight was heading straight for Genesis. In the moments before the light would illuminate their hiding place, Ea said quietly to Damika 'It has been an honour to serve with you…' Quietly without turning on the sensors Ea said 'Fire!'

Damika slammed the button once more and being so close to the front Tartaran ship, did not need the aid of the sensor to find the target. The missile flew straight to the target causing the Tartaran ship to explode into fragments in front of Genesis – lighting up the sky in front of them. The blast caused Genesis to smash into the cliff face where they had been hiding. Damika grabbed the seat where she was sitting to steady herself and she saw the immediate response from the Tartaran ships beside the ship that had just blown up. Missiles spurted from their firing chambers and Damika watched as the missiles streaked towards Genesis with a vague understanding that this was the end. Her sensors noted the missile as it struck their faithful ship. The extra ammunition on board Genesis caused a vast detonation. The two Tartaran ships flying towards Genesis could not stop in time and they exploded in a massive blast, lighting up the night sky in an impressive fireball. Gravity sucked the fiery fragments towards the earth beneath them.

With the destruction of Genesis, the survivors of the Tartaran fleet limped around the other side of the moon to reorganise their command structure as many of the leading officers had been killed in the attack.

Back in the caves, a newborn baby announced their arrival to the world.